Great Stories
of
O. Henry

O. Henry

Great Stories of O. Henry

Illustrated by Ellen Stoepel

AVENEL BOOKS

NEW YORK

This edition is for Mary Dickson

ISBN: 0-517-162237
Copyright © MCMLXXIV by Crown Publishers, Inc.
Library of Congress Catalog Card Number: 74-25076
All rights reserved.
This edition is published by Avenel Books,
a division of Barre Publishing Company, Inc.
        f g h
Manufactured in the United States of America

Frontispiece by Doug Anderson

Book designed by Joseph M. Regina

Contents

THE VOICE OF THE CITY

TWENTY-FIVE years ago the school children used to chant their lessons. The manner of their delivery was a singsong recitative between the utterance of an Episcopal minister and the drone of a tired sawmill. I mean no disrespect. We must have lumber and sawdust.

I remember one beautiful and instructive little lyric that emanated from the physiology class. The most striking line of it was this:

" The shin-bone is the long-est bone in the hu-man bod-y."

What an inestimable boon it would have been if all the corporeal and spiritual facts pertaining to man had thus been tunefully and logically inculcated in our youthful minds! But what we gained in anatomy, music and philosophy was meagre.

The other day I became confused. I needed a ray of light. I turned back to those school days for aid. But in all the nasal harmonies we whined forth from those hard benches I could not recall one that treated of the voice of agglomerated mankind.

In other words, of the composite vocal message of massed humanity.

In other words, of the Voice of a Big City.

Now, the individual voice is not lacking. We can understand the song of the poet, the ripple of the brook, the meaning of the man who wants $5 until next Monday, the inscriptions on the tombs of the Pharaohs, the language of flowers, the "step lively" of the conductor, and the prelude of the milk cans at 4 A. M. Certain large-eared ones even assert that they are wise to the vibrations of the tympanum produced by concussion of the air emanating from Mr. H. James. But who can comprehend the meaning of the voice of the city?

I went out for to see.

First, I asked Aurelia. She wore white Swiss and a hat with flowers on it, and ribbons and ends of things fluttered here and there.

"Tell me," I said, stammeringly, for I have no voice of my own, "what does this big — er — enormous — er — whopping city say? It must have a voice of some kind. Does it ever speak to you? How do you interpret its meaning? It is a tremendous mass, but it must have a key."

"Like a Saratoga trunk?" asked Aurelia.

"No," said I. "Please do not refer to the lid. I have a fancy that every city has a voice. Each one has something to say to the one who can hear it. What does the big one say to you?"

"All cities," said Aurelia, judicially, "say the

"She sat on the high stoop. A spray of insolent ivy bobbed against her ear."

same thing. When they get through saying it there is an echo from Philadelphia. So, they are unanimous."

" Here are 4,000,000 people," said I, scholastically, " compressed upon an island, which is mostly lamb surrounded by Wall Street water. The conjunction of so many units into so small a space must result in an identity — or, or rather a homogeneity — that finds its oral expression through a common channel. It is, as you might say, a consensus of translation, concentrating in a crystallized, general idea which reveals itself in what may be termed the Voice of the City. Can you tell me what it is? "

Aurelia smiled wonderfully. She sat on the high stoop. A spray of insolent ivy bobbed against her right ear. A ray of impudent moonlight flickered upon her nose. But I was adamant, nickel-plated.

" I must go and find out," I said, " what is the Voice of this city. Other cities have voices. It is an assignment. I must have it. New York," I continued, in a rising tone, " had better not hand me a cigar and say : ' Old man, I can't talk for publication.' No other city acts in that way. Chicago says, unhesitatingly, ' I will ; ' Philadelphia says, ' I should ; ' New Orleans says, ' I used to ; ' Louisville says, ' Don't care if I do ; ' St. Louis says, ' Excuse me ; ' Pittsburg says, ' Smoke up.' Now, New York ——"

Aurelia smiled.

" Very well," said I, " I must go elsewhere and find out."

I went into a palace, tile-floored, cherub-ceilinged and square with the cop. I put my foot on the brass rail and said to Billy Magnus, the best bartender in the diocese:

" Billy, you've lived in New York a long time — what kind of a song-and-dance does this old town give you? What I mean is, doesn't the gab of it seem to kind of bunch up and slide over the bar to you in a sort of amalgamated tip that hits off the burg in a kind of an epigram with a dash of bitters and a slice of —— "

" Excuse me a minute," said Billy, " somebody's punching the button at the side door."

He went away; came back with an empty tin bucket; again vanished with it full; returned and said to me:

" That was Mame. She rings twice. She likes a glass of beer for supper. Her and the kid. If you ever saw that little skeesicks of mine brace up in his high chair and take his beer and —— But, say, what was yours? I get kind of excited when I hear them two rings — was it the baseball score or gin fizz you asked for? "

" Ginger ale," I answered.

I walked up to Broadway. I saw a cop on the corner. The cops take kids up, women across, and men in. I went up to him.

" If I'm not exceeding the spiel limit," I said, " let me ask you. You see New York during its vocative hours. It is the function of you and your brother cops to preserve the acoustics of the city. There must be a civic voice that is intelligible to you. At night during your lonely rounds you must have heard it. What is the epitome of its turmoil and shouting? What does the city say to you? "

" Friend," said the policeman, spinning his club, " it don't say nothing. I get my orders from the man higher up. Say, I guess you're all right. Stand here for a few minutes and keep an eye open for the roundsman."

The cop melted into the darkness of the side street. In ten minutes he had returned.

" Married last Tuesday," he said, half gruffly. " You know how they are. She comes to that corner at nine every night for a — comes to say ' hello ! ' I generally manage to be there. Say, what was it you asked me a bit ago — what's doing in the city? Oh, there's a roof-garden or two just opened, twelve blocks up."

I crossed a crow's-foot of street-car tracks, and skirted the edge of an umbrageous park. An artificial Diana, gilded, heroic, poised, wind-ruled, on the tower, shimmered in the clear light of her namesake in the sky. Along came my poet, hurrying, hatted, haired, emitting dactyls, spondees and dactylis. I seized him.

" Bill," said I (in the magazine he is Cleon), " give me a lift. I am on an assignment to find out the Voice of the city. You see, it's a special order. Ordinarily a symposium comprising the views of Henry Clews, John L. Sullivan, Edwin Markham, May Irwin and Charles Schwab would be about all. But this is a different matter. We want a broad, poetic, mystic vocalization of the city's soul and meaning. You are the very chap to give me a hint. Some years ago a man got at the Niagara Falls and gave us its pitch. The note was about two feet below the lowest G on the piano. Now, you can't put New York into a note unless it's better indorsed than that. But give me an idea of what it would say if it should speak. It is bound to be a mighty and far-reaching utterance. To arrive at it we must take the tremendous crash of the chords of the day's traffic, the laughter and music of the night, the solemn tones of Dr. Parkhurst, the rag-time, the weeping, the stealthy hum of cab-wheels, the shout of the press agent, the tinkle of fountains on the roof gardens, the hullabaloo of the strawberry vender and the covers of *Everybody's Magazine*, the whispers of the lovers in the parks — all these sounds must go into your Voice — not combined, but mixed, and of the mixture an essence made; and of the essence an extract — an audible extract, of which one drop shall form the thing we seek."

"Do you remember," asked the poet, with a chuckle, "that California girl we met at Stiver's studio last week? Well, I'm on my way to see her. She repeated that poem of mine, 'The Tribute of Spring,' word for word. She's the smartest proposition in this town just at present. Say, how does this confounded tie look? I spoiled four before I got one to set right."

"And the Voice that I asked you about?" I inquired.

"Oh, she doesn't sing," said Cleon. "But you ought to hear her recite my 'Angel of the Inshore Wind.'"

I passed on. I cornered a newsboy and he flashed at me prophetic pink papers that outstripped the news by two revolutions of the clock's longest hand.

"Son," I said, while I pretended to chase coins in my penny pocket, "doesn't it sometimes seem to you as if the city ought to be able to talk? All these ups and downs and funny business and queer things happening every day — what would it say, do you think, if it could speak?"

"Quit yer kiddin'," said the boy. "Wot paper yer want? I got no time to waste. It's Mag's birthday, and I want thirty cents to git her a present."

Here was no interpreter of the city's mouthpiece.

I bought a paper, and consigned its undeclared treaties, its premeditated murders and unfought battles to an ash can.

Again I repaired to the park and sat in the moon shade. I thought and thought, and wondered why none could tell me what I asked for.

And then, as swift as light from a fixed star, the answer came to me. I arose and hurried — hurried as so many reasoners must, back around my circle. I knew the answer and I hugged it in my breast as I flew, fearing lest some one would stop me and demand my secret.

Aurelia was still on the stoop. The moon was higher and the ivy shadows were deeper. I sat at her side and we watched a little cloud tilt at the drifting moon and go asunder, quite pale and discomfited.

And then, wonder of wonders and delight of delights! our hands somehow touched, and our fingers closed together and did not part.

After half an hour Aurelia said, with that smile of hers:

"Do you know, you haven't spoken a word since you came back!"

"That," said I, nodding wisely, "is the Voice of the City."

ONE THOUSAND DOLLARS

ONE thousand dollars," repeated Lawyer Tolman, solemnly and severely, " and here is the money."

Young Gillian gave a decidedly amused laugh as he fingered the thin package of new fifty-dollar notes.

" It's such a confoundedly awkward amount," he explained, genially, to the lawyer. " If it had been ten thousand a fellow might wind up with a lot of fireworks and do himself credit. Even fifty dollars would have been less trouble."

" You heard the reading of your uncle's will," continued Lawyer Tolman, professionally dry in his tones. " I do not know if you paid much attention to its details. I must remind you of one. You are required to render to us an account of the manner of expenditure of this $1,000 as soon as you have disposed of it. The will stipulates that. I trust that you will so far comply with the late Mr. Gillian's wishes."

" You may depend upon it," said the young man, politely, " in spite of the extra expense it will entail. I may have to engage a secretary. I was never good at accounts."

Gillian went to his club. There he hunted out one whom he called Old Bryson.

Old Bryson was calm and forty and sequestered. He was in a corner reading a book, and when he saw Gillian approaching he sighed, laid down his book and took off his glasses.

"Old Bryson, wake up," said Gillian. "I've a funny story to tell you."

"I wish you would tell it to some one in the billiard room," said Old Bryson. "You know how I hate your stories."

"This is a better one than usual," said Gillian rolling a cigarette; "and I'm glad to tell it to you. It's too sad and funny to go with the rattling of billiard balls. I've just come from my late uncle's firm of legal corsairs. He leaves me an even thousand dollars. Now, what can a man possibly do with a thousand dollars?"

"I thought," said Old Bryson, showing as much interest as a bee shows in a vinegar cruet, "that the late Septimus Gillian was worth something like half a million."

"He was," assented Gillian, joyously, "and that's where the joke comes in. He's left his whole cargo of doubloons to a microbe. That is, part of it goes to the man who invents a new bacillus and the rest to establish a hospital for doing away with it again. There are one or two trifling bequests on the side. The butler and the housekeeper get a seal ring and $10 each. His nephew gets $1,000."

" You've always had plenty of money to spend," observed Old Bryson.

" Tons," said Gillian. " Uncle was the fairygodmother as far as an allowance was concerned."

" Any other heirs? " asked Old Bryson.

" None." Gillian frowned at his cigarette and kicked the upholstered leather of a divan uneasily. " There is a Miss Hayden, a ward of my uncle, who lived in his house. She's a quiet thing — musical — the daughter of somebody who was unlucky enough to be his friend. I forgot to say that she was in on the seal ring and $10 joke, too. I wish I had been. Then I could have had two bottles of brut, tipped the waiter with the ring and had the whole business off my hands. Don't be superior and insulting, Old Bry son — tell me what a fellow can do with a thousand dollars."

Old Bryson rubbed his glasses and smiled. And when Old Bryson smiled, Gillian knew that he intended to be more offensive than ever.

" A thousand dollars," he said, " means much or little. One man may buy a happy home with it and laugh at Rockefeller. Another could send his wife South with it and save her life. A thousand dollars would buy pure milk for one hundred babies during June, July, and August and save fifty of their lives. You could count upon a half hour's diversion with it at faro in one of the fortified art galleries. It would furnish an education to an ambitious boy. I am told that a genuine Corot was secured for that amount in an auction room yesterday. You could move to a New Hampshire town and live respectably two years on it. You could rent Madison Square Garden for one evening with it, and lecture your audience, if you should have one, on the precariousness of the profession of heir presumptive."

" People might like you, Old Bryson," said Gillian, always unruffled, " if you wouldn't moralize. I asked you to tell me what I could do with a thousand dollars."

" You? " said Bryson, with a gentle laugh. " Why, Bobby Gillian, there's only one logical thing you could do. You can go buy Miss Lotta Lauriere a diamond pendant with the money, and then take yourself off to Idaho and inflict your presence upon a ranch. I advise a sheep ranch, as I have a particular dislike for sheep."

" Thanks," said Gillian, rising, " I thought I could depend upon you, Old Bryson. You've hit on the very scheme. I wanted to chuck the money in a lump, for I've got to turn in an account for it, and I hate itemizing."

Gillian phoned for a cab and said to the driver:

" The stage entrance of the Columbine Theatre."

Miss Lotta Lauriere was assisting nature with a powder puff, almost ready for her call at a crowded matinée, when her dresser mentioned the name of Mr. Gillian.

" Let it in," said Miss Lauriere. " Now, what is it, Bobby? I'm going on in two minutes."

" Rabbit-foot your right ear a little," suggested Gillian, critically. " That's better. It won't take two minutes for me. What do you say to a little thing in the pendant line? I can stand three ciphers with a figure one in front of 'em."

" Oh, just as you say," carolled Miss Lauriere. " My right glove, Adams. Say, Bobby, did you see that necklace Della Stacey had on the other night? Twenty-two hundred dollars it cost at Tiffany's. But, of course — pull my sash a little to the left, Adams."

" Miss Lauriere for the opening chorus ! " cried the call boy without.

Gillian strolled out to where his cab was waiting.

" What would you do with a thousand dollars if you had it ? " he asked the driver.

" Open a s'loon," said the cabby, promptly and huskily. " I know a place I could take money in with both hands. It's a four-story brick on a corner. I've got it figured out. Second story — Chinks and chop suey ; third floor — manicures and foreign missions ; fourth floor — poolroom. If you was thinking of putting up the cap —— "

" Oh, no," said Gillian, " I merely asked from curiosity. I take you by the hour. Drive till I tell you to stop."

Eight blocks down Broadway Gillian poked up the trap with his cane and got out. A blind man sat upon a stool on the sidewalk selling pencils. Gillian went out and stood before him.

" Excuse me," he said, " but would you mind telling me what you would do if you had a thousand dollars? "

" You got out of that cab that just drove up, didn't you? " asked the blind man.

" I did," said Gillian.

" I guess you are all right," said the pencil dealer, " to ride in a cab by daylight. Take a look at that, if you like."

He drew a small book from his coat pocket and held it out. Gillian opened it and saw that it was a bank deposit book. It showed a balance of $1,785 to the blind man's credit.

Gillian returned the book and got into the cab.

" I forgot something," he said. " You may drive to the law offices of Tolman & Sharp, at —— Broadway."

Lawyer Tolman looked at him hostilely and inquiringly through his gold-rimmed glasses.

" I beg your pardon," said Gillian, cheerfully, " but may I ask you a question? It is not an impertinent one, I hope. Was Miss Hayden left any thing by my uncle's will besides the ring and the $10? "

" Nothing," said Mr. Tolman.

" I thank you very much, sir," said Gillian, and out he went to his cab. He gave the driver the address of his late uncle's home.

Miss Hayden was writing letters in the library. She was small and slender and clothed in black. But you would have noticed her eyes. Gillian drifted in with his air of regarding the world as inconsequent.

" I've just come from old Tolman's," he explained. " They've been going over the papers down there. They found a " — Gillian searched his memory for a legal term — " they found an amendment or a postscript or something to the will. It seemed that the old boy loosened up a little on second thoughts and willed you a thousand dollars. I was driving up this way and Tolman asked me to bring you the money. Here it is. You'd better count it to see if it's right." Gillian laid the money beside her hand on the desk.

Miss Hayden turned white. " Oh! " she said, and again " Oh! "

Gillian half turned and looked out the window.

" I suppose, of course," he said, in a low voice, " that you know I love you."

" I am sorry," said Miss Hayden, taking up her money.

"She was small and slender and clothed in black. But you would have noticed her eyes."

" There is no use? " asked Gillian, almost light-heartedly.

" I am sorry," she said again.

" May I write a note? " asked Gillian, with a smile. He seated himself at the big library table. She supplied him with paper and pen, and then went back to her secrétaire.

Gillian made out his account of his expenditure of the thousand dollars in these words:

" Paid by the black sheep, Robert Gillian, $1,000 on account of the eternal happiness, owed by Heaven to the best and dearest woman on earth."

Gillian slipped his writing into an envelope, bowed and went his way.

His cab stopped again at the offices of Tolman & Sharp.

" I have expended the thousand dollars," he said, cheerily, to Tolman of the gold glasses, " and I have come to render account of it, as I agreed. There is quite a feeling of summer in the air — do you not think so, Mr. Tolman? " He tossed a white envelope on the lawyer's table. " You will find there a memorandum, sir, of the *modus operandi* of the vanishing of the dollars."

Without touching the envelope, Mr. Tolman went to a door and called his partner, Sharp. Together they explored the caverns of an immense safe. Forth they dragged as trophy of their search a big envelope sealed with wax. This they forcibly invaded, and wagged their venerable heads together over its contents. Then Tolman became spokesman.

" Mr. Gillian," he said, formally, " there was a codicil to your uncle's will. It was intrusted to us privately, with instructions that it be not opened until you had furnished us with a full account of your handling of the $1,000 bequest in the will. As you have fulfilled the conditions, my partner and I have read the codicil. I do not wish to encumber your understanding with its legal phraseology, but I will acquaint you with the spirit of its contents.

" In the event that your disposition of the $1,000 demonstrates that you possess any of the qualifications that deserve reward, much benefit will accrue to you. Mr. Sharp and I are named as the judges, and I assure you that we will do our duty strictly according to justice — with liberality. We are not at all unfavorably disposed toward you, Mr. Gillian. But let us return to the letter of the codicil. If your disposal of the money in question has been prudent, wise, or unselfish, it is in our power to hand you over bonds to the value of $50,000, which have been placed in our hands for that purpose. But if — as our client, the late Mr. Gillian, explicitly provides — you have used this money as you have used money in the past — I quote the late Mr. Gillian — in reprehensible dissipation among disreputable

associates — the $50,000 is to be paid to Miriam
Hayden, ward of the late Mr. Gillian, without delay.
Now, Mr. Gillian, Mr. Sharp and I will examine your
account in regard to the $1,000. You submit it in
writing, I believe. I hope you will repose confidence
in our decision."

Mr. Tolman reached for the envelope. Gillian
was a little the quicker in taking it up. He tore the
account and its cover leisurely into strips and dropped
them into his pocket.

" It's all right," he said, smilingly. " There isn't a
bit of need to bother you with this. I don't suppose
you'd understand these itemized bets, anyway. I
lost the thousand dollars on the races. Good-day to
you, gentlemen."

Tolman & Sharp shook their heads mournfully at
each other when Gillian left, for they heard him whistling gayly in the hallway as he waited for the ele-
vator.

THE TRIMMED LAMP

Of course there are two sides to the question. Let us look at the other. We often hear " shop-girls " spoken of. No such persons exist. There are girls who work in shops. They make their living that way. But why turn their occupation into an adjective? Let us be fair. We do not refer to the girls who live on Fifth Avenue as " marriage-girls."

Lou and Nancy were chums. They came to the big city to find work because there was not enough to eat at their homes to go around. Nancy was nineteen; Lou was twenty. Both were pretty, active, country girls who had no ambition to go on the stage.

The little cherub that sits up aloft guided them to a cheap and respectable boarding-house. Both found positions and became wage-earners. They remained chums. It is at the end of six months that I would beg you to step forward and be introduced to them. Meddlesome Reader: My Lady friends, Miss Nancy and Miss Lou. While you are shaking hands please take notice — cautiously — of their attire. Yes, cautiously; for they are as quick to resent a stare as a lady in a box at the horse show is.

Lou is a piece-work ironer in a hand laundry. She

is clothed in a badly-fitting purple dress, and her hat plume is four inches too long; but her ermine muff and scarf cost $25, and its fellow beasts will be ticketed in the windows at $7.98 before the season is over. Her cheeks are pink, and her light blue eyes bright. Contentment radiates from her.

Nancy you would call a shop-girl — because you have the habit. There is no type; but a perverse generation is always seeking a type; so this is what the type should be. She has the high-ratted pompadour, and the exaggerated straight-front. Her skirt is shoddy, but has the correct flare. No furs protect her against the bitter spring air, but she wears her short broadcloth jacket as jauntily as though it were Persian lamb! On her face and in her eyes, remorseless type-seeker, is the typical shop-girl expression. It is a look of silent but contemptuous revolt against cheated womanhood; of sad prophecy of the vengeance to come. When she laughs her loudest the look is still there. The same look can be seen in the eyes of Russian peasants; and those of us left will see it some day on Gabriel's face when he comes to blow us up. It is a look that should wither and abash man; but he has been known to smirk at it and offer flowers — with a string tied to them.

Now lift your hat and come away, while you receive Lou's cheery " See you again," and the sardonic, sweet smile of Nancy that seems, somehow, to miss you and go fluttering like a white moth up over the house-tops to the stars.

The two waited on the corner for Dan. Dan was Lou's steady company. Faithful? Well, he was on hand when Mary would have had to hire a dozen subpoena servers to find her lamb.

"Ain't you cold, Nance?" said Lou. "Say, what a chump you are for working in that old store for $8. a week! I made $18.50 last week. Of course ironing ain't as swell work as selling lace behind a counter, but it pays. None of us ironers make less than $10. And I don't know that it's any less respectful work, either."

"You can have it," said Nancy, with uplifted nose. "I'll take my eight a week and hall bedroom. I like to be among nice things and swell people. And look what a chance I've got! Why, one of our glove girls married a Pittsburg — steel maker, or blacksmith or something — the other day worth a million dollars. I'll catch a swell myself some time. I ain't bragging on my looks or anything; but I'll take my chances where there's big prizes offered. What show would a girl have in a laundry?"

"Why, that's where I met Dan," said Lou, triumphantly. "He came in for his Sunday shirt and collars and saw me at the first board, ironing. We all try to get to work at the first board. Ella Maginnis was sick that day, and I had her place. He said he noticed my arms first, how round and white they was. I had my sleeves rolled up. Some nice fellows come into laundries. You can tell 'em by their bringing their clothes in suit cases, and turning in the door sharp and sudden."

" How can you wear a waist like that, Lou? " said Nancy, gazing down at the offending article with sweet scorn in her heavy-lidded eyes. " It shows fierce taste."

" This waist? " cried Lou, with wide-eyed indignation. " Why, I paid $16. for this waist. It's worth twenty-five. A woman left it to be laundered, and never called for it. The boss sold it to me. It's got yards and yards of hand embroidery on it. Better talk about that ugly, plain thing you've got on."

" This ugly, plain thing," said Nancy, calmly, " was copied from one that Mrs. Van Alstyne Fisher was wearing. The girls say her bill in the store last year was $12,000. I made mine, myself. It cost me $1.50. Ten feet away you couldn't tell it from hers."

" Oh, well," said Lou, good-naturedly, " if you want to starve and put on airs, go ahead. But I'll take my job and good wages; and after hours give me something as fancy and attractive to wear as I am able to buy."

But just then Dan came — a serious young man

"How can you wear a waist like that, Lou? It shows fierce taste."

with a ready-made necktie, who had escaped the city's brand of frivolity — an electrician earning $30. per week who looked upon Lou with the sad eyes of Romeo, and thought her embroidered waist a web in which any fly should delight to be caught.

" My friend, Mr. Owens — shake hands with Miss Danforth," said Lou.

" I'm mighty glad to know you, Miss Danforth," said Dan, with outstretched hand. " I've heard Lou speak of you so often."

" Thanks," said Nancy, touching his fingers with the tips of her cool ones, " I've heard her mention you — a few times."

Lou giggled.

" Did you get that handshake from Mrs. Van Alstyne Fisher, Nance? " she asked.

" If I did, you can feel safe in copying it," said Nancy.

" Oh, I couldn't use it at all. It's too stylish for me. It's intended to set off diamond rings, that high shake is. Wait till I get a few and then I'll try it."

" Learn it first," said Nancy wisely, " and you'll be more likely to get the rings."

" Now, to settle this argument," said Dan, with his ready, cheerful smile, " let me make a proposition. As I can't take both of you up to Tiffany's and do the right thing, what do you say to a little vaudeville? I've got the tickets. How about looking at stage dia-

monds since we can't shake hands with the real spark-
lers?"

The faithful squire took his place close to the curb;
Lou next, a little peacocky in her bright and pretty
clothes; Nancy on the inside, slender, and soberly
clothed as the sparrow, but with the true Van Alstyne
Fisher walk — thus they set out for their evening's
moderate diversion.

I do not suppose that many look upon a great department store as an educational institution. But the
one in which Nancy worked was something like that to
her. She was surrounded by beautiful things that
breathed of taste and refinement. If you live in an
atmosphere of luxury, luxury is yours whether your
money pays for it, or another's.

The people she served were mostly women whose
dress, manners, and position in the social world were
quoted as criterions. From them Nancy began to
take toll — the best from each according to her view.

From one she would copy and practice a gesture,
from another an eloquent lifting of an eyebrow, from
others, a manner of walking, of carrying a purse, of
smiling, of greeting a friend, of addressing " inferiors
in station." From her best beloved model, Mrs. Van
Alstyne Fisher, she made requisition for that excellent
thing, a soft, low voice as clear as silver and as per-
fect in articulation as the notes of a thrush. Suffused
in the aura of this high social refinement and good

breeding, it was impossible for her to escape a deeper effect of it. As good habits are said to be better than good principles, so, perhaps, good manners are better than good habits. The teachings of your parents may not keep alive your New England conscience; but if you sit on a straight-back chair and repeat the words " prisms and pilgrims " forty times the devil will flee from you. And when Nancy spoke in the Van Alstyne Fisher tones she felt the thrill of *noblesse oblige* to her very bones.

There was another source of learning in the great departmental school. Whenever you see three or four shop-girls gather in a bunch and jingle their wire bracelets as an accompaniment to apparently frivolous conversation, do not think that they are there for the purpose of criticizing the way Ethel does her back hair. The meeting may lack the dignity of the deliberative bodies of man; but it has all the importance of the occasion on which Eve and her first daughter first put their heads together to make Adam understand his proper place in the household. It is Woman's Conference for Common Defense and Exchange of Strategical Theories of Attack and Repulse upon and against the World, which is a Stage, and Man, its Audience who Persists in Throwing Bouquets Thereupon. Woman, the most helpless of the young of any animal — with the fawn's grace but without its fleetness; with the bird's beauty but without its power of flight; with the honey-bee's burden of sweetness but without its — Oh, let's drop that simile — some of us may have been stung.

During this council of war they pass weapons one to another, and exchange stratagems that each has devised and formulated out of the tactics of life.

" I says to 'im," says Sadie, " ain't you the fresh thing! Who do you suppose I am, to be addressing such a remark to me? And what do you think he says back to me? "

The heads, brown, black, flaxen, red, and yellow bob together; the answer is given; and the parry to the thrust is decided upon, to be used by each thereafter in passages-at-arms with the common enemy, man.

Thus Nancy learned the art of defense; and to women successful defense means victory.

The curriculum of a department store is a wide one. Perhaps no other college could have fitted her as well for her life's ambition — the drawing of a matrimonial prize.

Her station in the store was a favored one. The music room was near enough for her to hear and become familiar with the works of the best composers — at least to acquire the familiarity that passed for appreciation in the social world in which she was vaguely trying to set a tentative and aspiring foot. She absorbed the educating influence of art wares, of costly and dainty fabrics, of adornments that are almost culture to women.

The other girls soon became aware of Nancy's ambition. "Here comes your millionaire, Nancy," they would call to her whenever any man who looked the rôle approached her counter. It got to be a habit of men, who were hanging about while their women folk were shopping, to stroll over to the handkerchief counter and dawdle over the cambric squares. Nancy's imitation high-bred air and genuine dainty beauty was what attracted. Many men thus came to display their graces before her. Some of them may have been millionaires; others were certainly no more than their sedulous apes. Nancy learned to discriminate. There was a window at the end of the handkerchief counter; and she could see the rows of vehicles waiting for the shoppers in the street below. She looked, and perceived that automobiles differ as well as do their owners.

Once a fascinating gentleman bought four dozen handkerchiefs, and wooed her across the counter with a King Cophetua air. When he had gone one of the girls said:

"What's wrong, Nance, that you didn't warm up to that fellow? He looks the swell article, all right, to me."

"Him?" said Nancy, with her coolest, sweetest, most impersonal, Van Alstyne Fisher smile; "not for mine. I saw him drive up outside. A 12 H. P. machine and an Irish chauffeur! And you saw what kind of handkerchiefs he bought — silk! And he's got dactylis on him. Give me the real thing or nothing, if you please."

Two of the most " refined " women in the store — a forelady and a cashier — had a few " swell gentlemen friends " with whom they now and then dined. Once they included Nancy in an invitation. The dinner took place in a spectacular café whose tables are engaged for New Year's eve a year in advance. There were two " gentlemen friends "— one without any hair on his head — high living ungrew it; and we can prove it — the other a young man whose worth and sophistication he impressed upon you in two convincing ways — he swore that all the wine was corked; and he wore diamond cuff buttons. This young man perceived irresistible excellencies in Nancy. His taste ran to shop-girls; and here was one that added the voice and manners of his high social world to the franker charms of her own caste. So, on the following day, he appeared in the store and made her a serious proposal of marriage over a box of hemstitched, grass-bleached Irish linens. Nancy declined. A brown pompadour ten feet away had been using her eyes and ears. When the rejected suitor had gone she heaped carboys of upbraidings and horror upon Nancy's head.

" What a terrible little fool you are! That fellow's
a millionaire — he's a nephew of old Van Skittles himself. And he was talking on the level, too. Have
you gone crazy, Nance? "

" Have I? " said Nancy. " I didn't take him, did
I? He isn't a millionaire so hard that you could notice it, anyhow. His family only allows him $20,000
a year to spend. The bald-headed fellow was guying
him about it the other night at supper."

The brown pompadour came nearer and narrowed
her eyes.

" Say, what do you want? " she inquired, in a voice
hoarse for lack of chewing-gum. " Ain't that enough
for you? Do you want to be a Mormon, and marry
Rockefeller and Gladstone Dowie and the King of
Spain and the whole bunch? Ain't $20,000 a year
good enough for you? "

Nancy flushed a little under the level gaze of the
black, shallow eyes.

" It wasn't altogether the money, Carrie," she explained. " His friend caught him in a rank lie the
other night at dinner. It was about some girl he said
he hadn't been to the theater with. Well, I can't stand
a liar. Put everything together — I don't like him;
and that settles it. When I sell out it's not going to
be on any bargain day. I've got to have something
that sits up in a chair like a man, anyhow. Yes, I'm
looking out for a catch; but it's got to be able to do

something more than make a noise like a toy bank."

"The physiopathic ward for yours!" said the brown pompadour, walking away.

These high ideas, if not ideals — Nancy continued to cultivate on $8. per week. She bivouacked on the trail of the great unknown "catch," eating her dry bread and tightening her belt day by day. On her face was the faint, soldierly, sweet, grim smile of the preordained man-hunter. The store was her forest; and many times she raised her rifle at game that seemed broad-antlered and big; but always some deep unerring instinct — perhaps of the huntress, perhaps of the woman — made her hold her fire and take up the trail again.

Lou flourished in the laundry. Out of her $18.50 per week she paid $6. for her room and board. The rest went mainly for clothes. Her opportunities for bettering her taste and manners were few compared with Nancy's. In the steaming laundry there was nothing but work, work and her thoughts of the evening pleasures to come. Many costly and showy fabrics passed under her iron; and it may be that her growing fondness for dress was thus transmitted to her throrgh the conducting metal.

When the day's work was over Dan awaited her outside, her faithful shadow in whatever light she stood.

Sometimes he cast an honest and troubled glance

at Lou's clothes that increased in conspicuity rather than in style; but this was no disloyalty; he deprecated the attention they called to her in the streets.

And Lou was no less faithful to her chum. There was a law that Nancy should go with them on whatsoever outings they might take. Dan bore the extra burden heartily and in good cheer. It might be said that Lou furnished the color, Nancy the tone, and Dan the weight of the distraction-seeking trio. The escort, in his neat but obviously ready-made suit, his ready-made tie and unfailing, genial, ready-made wit never startled or clashed. He was of that good kind that you are likely to forget while they are present, but remember distinctly after they are gone.

To Nancy's superior taste the flavor of these ready-made pleasures was sometimes a little bitter: but she was young; and youth is a gourmand, when it cannot be a gourmet.

" Dan is always wanting me to marry him right away," Lou told her once. " But why should I. I'm independent. I can do as I please with the money I earn; and he never would agree for me to keep on working afterward. And say, Nance, what do you want to stick to that old store for, and half starve and half dress yourself? I could get you a place in the laundry right now if you'd come. It seems to me that you could afford to be a little less stuck-up if you could make a good deal more money."

"I don't think I'm stuck-up, Lou," said Nancy, "but I'd rather live on half rations and stay where I am. I suppose I've got the habit. It's the chance that I want. I don't expect to be always behind a counter. I'm learning something new every day. I'm right up against refined and rich people all the time — even if I do only wait on them; and I'm not missing any pointers that I see passing around."

"Caught your millionaire yet?" asked Lou with her teasing laugh.

"I haven't selected one yet," answered Nancy. "I've been looking them over."

"Goodness! the idea of picking over 'em! Don't you ever let one get by you Nance — even if he's a few dollars shy. But of course you're joking — millionaires don't think about working girls like us."

"It might be better for them if they did," said Nancy, with cool wisdom. "Some of us could teach them how to take care of their money."

"If one was to speak to me," laughed Lou, "I know I'd have a duck-fit."

"That's because you don't know any. The only difference between swells and other people is you have to watch 'em closer. Don't you think that red silk lining is just a little bit too bright for that coat, Lou?"

Lou looked at the plain, dull olive jacket of her friend.

" Well, no I don't — but it may seem so beside that faded-looking thing you've got on."

" This jacket," said Nancy, complacently, " has exactly the cut and fit of one that Mrs. Van Alstyne Fisher was wearing the other day. The material cost me $3.98. I suppose hers cost about $100. more."

" Oh, well," said Lou lightly, " it don't strike me as millionaire bait. Shouldn't wonder if I catch one before you do, anyway."

Truly it would have taken a philosopher to decide upon the values of the theories held by the two friends. Lou, lacking that certain pride and fastidiousness that keeps stores and desks filled with girls working for the barest living, thumped away gaily with her iron in the noisy and stifling laundry. Her wages supported her even beyond the point of comfort; so that her dress profited until sometimes she cast a sidelong glance of impatience at the neat but inelegant apparel of Dan — Dan the constant, the immutable, the undeviating.

As for Nancy, her case was one of tens of thousands. Silk and jewels and laces and ornaments and the perfume and music of the fine world of good-breeding and taste — these were made for woman; they are her equitable portion. Let her keep near them if they are a part of life to her, and if she will. She is no traitor to herself, as Esau was; for she keeps her birthright and the pottage she earns is often very scant.

In this atmosphere Nancy belonged; and she throve in it and ate her frugal meals and schemed over her cheap dresses with a determined and contented mind. She already knew woman; and she was studying man, the animal, both as to his habits and eligibility. Some day she would bring down the game that she wanted; but she promised herself it would be what seemed to her the biggest and the best, and nothing smaller.

Thus she kept her lamp trimmed and burning to receive the bridegroom when he should come.

But, another lesson she learned, perhaps unconsciously. Her standard of values began to shift and change. Sometimes the dollar-mark grew blurred in her mind's eye, and shaped itself into letters that spelled such words as " truth " and " honor " and now and then just " kindness." Let us make a likeness of one who hunts the moose or elk in some mighty wood. He sees a little dell, mossy and embowered, where a rill trickles, babbling to him of rest and comfort. At these times the spear of Nimrod himself grows blunt.

So, Nancy wondered sometimes if Persian lamb was always quoted at its market value by the hearts that it covered.

One Thursday evening Nancy left the store and turned across Sixth Avenue westward to the laundry. She was expected to go with Lou and Dan to a musical comedy.

Dan was just coming out of the laundry when she

arrived.   There was a queer, strained look on his face.

" I thought I would drop around to see if they had
heard from her," he said.

" Heard from who? " asked Nancy.   " Isn't Lou
there? "

" I thought you knew," said Dan.   " She hasn't
been here or at the house where she lived since Mon-
day.   She moved all her things from there.   She told
one of the girls in the laundry she might be going to
Europe."

" Hasn't anybody seen her anywhere? " asked
Nancy.

Dan looked at her with his jaws set grimly, and a
steely gleam in his steady gray eyes.

" They told me in the laundry," he said, harshly,
" that they saw her pass yesterday — in an automobile.   With one of the millionaires, I suppose, that
you and Lou were forever busying your brains about."

For the first time Nancy quailed before a man.
She laid her hand that trembled slightly on Dan's
sleeve.

" You've no right to say such a thing to me, Dan
— as if I had anything to do with it! "

" I didn't mean it that way," said Dan, softening.
He fumbled in his vest pocket.

" I've got the tickets for the show to-night," he
said, with a gallant show of lightness.   " If you —"

Nancy admired pluck whenever she saw it.

" I'll go with you, Dan," she said.

Three months went by before Nancy saw Lou again.

At twilight one evening the shop-girl was hurrying home along the border of a little quiet park. She heard her name called, and wheeled about in time to catch Lou rushing into her arms.

After the first embrace they drew their heads back as serpents do, ready to attack or to charm, with a thousand questions trembling on their swift tongues. And then Nancy noticed that prosperity had descended upon Lou, manifesting itself in costly furs, flashing gems, and creations of the tailors' art.

" You little fool! " cried Lou, loudly and affectionately. " I see you are still working in that store, and as shabby as ever. And how about that big catch you were going to make — nothing doing yet, I suppose? "

And then Lou looked, and saw that something better than prosperity had descended upon Nancy — something that shone brighter than gems in her eyes and redder than a rose in her cheeks, and that danced like electricity anxious to be loosed from the tip of her tongue.

" Yes, I'm still in the store," said Nancy, " but I'm going to leave it next week. I've made my catch — the biggest catch in the world. You won't mind now Lou, will you? — I'm going to be married to Dan — to Dan! — he's my Dan now — why, Lou! "

Around the corner of the park strolled one of those
new-crop, smooth-faced young policemen that are
making the force more endurable — at least to the
eye. He saw a woman with an expensive fur coat and
diamond-ringed hands crouching down against the
iron fence of the park sobbing turbulently, while a
slender, plainly-dressed working girl leaned close, trying to console her. But the Gibsonian cop, being of
the new order, passed on, pretending not to notice,
for he was wise enough to know that these matters
are beyond help, so far as the power he represents is
concerned, though he rap the pavement with his night-
stick till the sound goes up to the furthermost stars.

A MADISON SQUARE ARABIAN NIGHT

To Carson Chalmers, in his apartment near the square, Phillips brought the evening mail. Besides the routine correspondence there were two items bearing the same foreign postmark.

One of the incoming parcels contained a photograph of a woman. The other contained an interminable letter, over which Chalmers hung, absorbed, for a long time. The letter was from another woman; and it contained poisoned barbs, sweetly dipped in honey, and feathered with innuendoes concerning the photographed woman.

Chalmers tore this letter into a thousand bits and began to wear out his expensive rug by striding back and forth upon it. Thus an animal from the jungle acts when it is caged, and thus a caged man acts when he is housed in a jungle of doubt.

By and by the restless mood was overcome. The rug was not an enchanted one. For sixteen feet he could travel along it; three thousand miles was beyond its power to aid.

Phillips appeared. He never entered; he invariably appeared, like a well-oiled genie.

" Will you dine here, sir, or out? " he asked.

"Here," said Chalmers, "and in half an hour." He listened glumly to the January blasts making an Aeolian trombone of the empty street.

"Wait," he said to the disappearing genie. "As I came home across the end of the square I saw many men standing there in rows. There was one mounted upon something, talking. Why do those men stand in rows, and why are they there?"

"They are homeless men, sir," said Phillips. "The man standing on the box tries to get lodging for them for the night. People come around to listen and give him money. Then he sends as many as the money will pay for to some lodging-house. That is why they stand in rows; they get sent to bed in order as they come."

"By the time dinner is served," said Chalmers, "have one of those men here. He will dine with me."

"W-w-which —," began Phillips, stammering for the first time during his service.

"Choose one at random," said Chalmers. "You might see that he is reasonably sober — and a certain amount of cleanliness will not be held against him. That is all."

It was an unusual thing for Carson Chalmers to play the Caliph. But on that night he felt the inefficacy of conventional antidotes to melancholy.

Something wanton and egregious, something high-flavored and Arabian, he must have to lighten his mood.

On the half hour Phillips had finished his duties as slave of the lamp. The waiters from the restaurant below had whisked aloft the delectable dinner. The dining table, laid for two, glowed cheerily in the glow of the pink-shaded candles.

And now Phillips, as though he ushered a cardinal — or held in charge a burglar — wafted in the shivering guest who had been haled from the line of mendicant lodgers.

It is a common thing to call such men wrecks; if the comparison be used here it is the specific one of a derelict come to grief through fire. Even yet some flickering combustion illuminated the drifting hulk. His face and hands has been recently washed — a rite insisted upon by Phillips as a memorial to the slaughtered conventions. In the candle-light he stood, a flaw in the decorous fittings of the apartment. His face was a sickly white, covered almost to the eyes with a stubble the shade of a red Irish setter's coat. Phillips's comb had failed to control the pale brown hair, long matted and conformed to the contour of a constantly worn hat. His eyes were full of a hopeless, tricky defiance like that seen in a cur's that is cornered by his tormentors. His shabby coat was buttoned high, but a quarter inch of redeeming collar showed

above it. His manner was singularly free from em-
barrassment when Chalmers rose from his chair across
the round dining table.

" If you will oblige me," said the host, " I will be
glad to have your company at dinner."

" My name is Plumer," said the highway guest, in
harsh and aggressive tones.   " If you're like me, you
like to know the name of the party you're dining
with."

" I was going on to say," continued Chalmers
somewhat hastily, " that mine is Chalmers. Will
you sit opposite? "

Plumer, of the ruffled plumes, bent his knee for
Phillips to slide the chair beneath him. He had an
air of having sat at attended boards before. Phillips
set out the anchovies and olives.

" Good! " barked Plumer; " Going to be in courses,
is it? All right, my jovial ruler of Bagdad. I'm
your Scheherezade all the way to the toothpicks.
You're the first Caliph with a genuine Oriental flavor
I've struck since frost. What luck! And I was
forty-third in line. I finished counting, just as your
welcome emissary arrived to bid me to the feast. I
had about as much chance of getting a bed to-night
as I have of being the next President. How will you
have the sad story of my life, Mr. Al Raschid — a
chapter with each course or the whole edition with the
cigars and coffee? "

"The situation does not seem a novel one to you," said Chalmers with a smile.

"By the chin whiskers of the prophet — no!" answered the guest. "New York's as full of cheap Haroun al Raschids as Bagdad is of fleas. I've been held up for my story with a loaded meal pointed at my head twenty times. Catch anybody in New York giving you something for nothing! They spell curiosity and charity with the same set of building blocks. Lots of 'em will stake you to a dime and chop-suey; and a few of 'em will play Caliph to the tune of a top sirloin; but every one of 'em will stand over you till they screw your autobiography out of you with foot notes, appendix and unpublished fragments. Oh, I know what to do when I see victuals coming toward me in little old Bagdad-on-the-Subway. I strike the asphalt three times with my forehead and get ready to spiel yarns for my supper. I claim descent from the late Tommy Tucker, who was forced to hand out vocal harmony for his pre-digested wheaterina and spoopju."

"I do not ask your story," said Chalmers. "I tell you frankly that it was a sudden whim that prompted me to send for some stranger to dine with me. I assure you you will not suffer through any curiosity of mine."

"Oh, fudge!" exclaimed the guest, enthusiastically tackling his soup; "I don't mind it a bit. I'm a reg-

ular Oriental magazine with a red cover and the leaves
cut when the Caliph walks abroad. In fact, we fellows in the bed line have a sort of union rate for
things of this sort. Somebody's always stopping and
wanting to know what brought us down so low in the
world. For a sandwich and a glass of beer I tell 'em
that drink did it. For corned beef and cabbage and
a cup of coffee I give 'em the hard-hearted-landlord —
six-months-in-the-hospital-lost-job story. A sirloin
steak and a quarter for a bed gets the Wall Street
tragedy of the swept-away fortune and the gradual
descent. This is the first spread of this kind I've
stumbled against. I haven't got a story to fit it. I'll
tell you what, Mr. Chalmers, I'm going to tell you the
truth for this, if you'll listen to it. It'll be harder
for you to believe than the made-up ones."

An hour later the Arabian guest lay back with a
sigh of satisfaction while Phillips brought the coffee
and cigars and cleared the table.

"Did you ever hear of Sherrard Plumer?" he
asked, with a strange smile.

"I remember the name," said Chalmers. "He was
a painter, I think, of a good deal of prominence a
few years ago."

"Five years," said the guest. "Then I went down
like a chunk of lead. I'm Sherrard Plumer! I sold
the last portrait I painted for $2,000. After that I
couldn't have found a sitter for a gratis picture."

"What was the trouble?" Chalmers could not resist asking.

"Funny thing," answered Plumer, grimly. "Never quite understood it myself. For a while I swam like a cork. I broke into the swell crowd and got commissions right and left. The newspapers called me a fashionable painter. Then the funny things began to happen. Whenever I finished a picture people would come to see it, and whisper and look queerly at one another.

"I soon found out what the trouble was. I had a knack of bringing out in the face of a portrait the hidden character of the original. I don't know how I did it — I painted what I saw — but I know it did me. Some of my sitters were fearfully enraged and refused their pictures. I painted the portrait of a very beautiful and popular society dame. When it was finished her husband looked at it with a peculiar expression on his face, and the next week he sued for divorce.

"I remember one case of a prominent banker who sat to me. While I had his portrait on exhibition in my studio an acquaintance of his came in to look at it. 'Bless me,' says he, 'does he really look like that?' I told him it was considered a faithful likeness. 'I never noticed that expression about his eyes before,' said he; 'I think I'll drop downtown and change my bank account.' He did drop down, but the bank account was gone and so was Mr. Banker.

"It wasn't long till they put me out of business. People don't want their secret meannesses shown up in a picture. They can smile and twist their own faces and deceive you, but the picture can't. I couldn't get an order for another picture, and I had to give up. I worked as a newspaper artist for a while, and then for a lithographer, but my work with them got me into the same trouble. If I drew from a photograph my drawing showed up characteristics and expressions that you couldn't find in the photo, but I guess they were in the original, all right. The customers raised lively rows, especially the women, and I never could hold a job long. So I began to rest my weary head upon the breast of Old Booze for comfort. And pretty soon I was in the free-bed line and doing oral fiction for hand-outs among the food bazaars. Does the truthful statement weary thee, O Caliph? I can turn on the Wall Street disaster stop if you prefer, but that requires a tear, and I'm afraid I can't hustle one up after that good dinner."

"No, no," said Chalmers, earnestly, "you interest me very much. Did all of your portraits reveal some unpleasant trait, or were there some that did not suffer from the ordeal of your peculiar brush?"

"Some? Yes," said Plumer. "Children generally, a good many women and a sufficient number of men. All people aren't bad, you know. When they

were all right the pictures were all right. As I said,
I don't explain it, but I'm telling you facts."

On Chalmers's writing-table lay the photograph
that he had received that day in the foreign mail.
Ten minutes later he had Plumer at work making a
sketch from it in pastels. At the end of an hour the
artist rose and stretched wearily.

"It's done," he yawned. "You'll excuse me for
being so long. I got interested in the job. Lordy!
but I'm tired. No bed last night, you know. Guess
it'll have to be good night now, O Commander of the
Faithful!"

Chalmers went as far as the door with him and
slipped some bills into his hand.

"Oh! I'll take 'em," said Plumer. "All that's included in the fall. Thanks. And for the very good
dinner. I shall sleep on feathers to-night and dream
of Bagdad. I hope it won't turn out to be a dream
in the morning. Farewell, most excellent Caliph!"

Again Chalmers paced restlessly upon his rug. But
his beat lay as far from the table whereon lay the
pastel sketch as the room would permit. Twice, thrice,
he tried to approach it, but failed. He could see the
dun and gold and brown of the colors, but there was
a wall about it built by his fears that kept him at a
distance. He sat down and tried to calm himself.
He sprang up and rang for Phillips.

"There is a young artist in this building," he said,

"— a Mr. Reineman — do you know which is his apartment? "

" Top floor, front, sir," said Phillips.

" Go up and ask him to favor me with his presence here for a few minutes."

Reineman came at once. Chalmers introduced himself.

" Mr. Reineman," said he, " there is a little pastel sketch on yonder table. I would be glad if you will give me your opinion of it as to its artistic merits and as a picture."

The young artist advanced to the table and took up the sketch. Chalmers half turned away, leaning upon the back of a chair.

" How — do — you — find it? " he asked, slowly.

" As a drawing," said the artist, " I can't praise it enough. It's the work of a master — bold and fine and true. It puzzles me a little; I haven't seen any pastel work near as good in years."

" The face, man — the subject — the original — what would you say of that? "

" The face," said Reineman, " is the face of one of God's own angels. May I ask who —"

" My wife! " shouted Chalmers, wheeling and pouncing upon the astonished artist, gripping his hand and pounding his back. " She is traveling in Europe. Take that sketch, boy, and paint the picture of your life from it and leave the price to me."

"Ten minutes later he had Plumer at work making a sketch from it in pastels."

THE RUBAIYAT OF A SCOTCH HIGHBALL

THIS document is intended to strike somewhere between a temperance lecture and the " Bartender's Guide." Relative to the latter, drink shall swell the theme and be set forth in abundance. Agreeably to the former, not an elbow shall be crooked.

Bob Babbitt was " off the stuff." Which means — as you will discover by referring to the unabridged dictionary of Bohemia — that he had " cut out the booze; " that he was " on the water wagon." The reason for Bob's sudden attitude of hostility toward the " demon rum "— as the white ribboners miscall whiskey (see the " Bartender's Guide "), should be of interest to reformers and saloon-keepers.

There is always hope for a man who, when sober, will not concede or acknowledge that he was ever drunk. But when a man will say (in the apt words of the phrase-distiller), " I had a beautiful skate on last night," you will have to put stuff in his coffee as well as pray for him.

One evening on his way home Babbitt dropped in at the Broadway bar that he liked best. Always there were three or four fellows there from the downtown offices whom he knew. And then there would be highballs and stories, and he would hurry home to dinner a little late but feeling good, and a little sorry for the poor Standard Oil Company. On this evening as he entered he heard some one say: " Babbitt was in last night as full as a boiled owl."

Babbitt walked to the bar, and saw in the mirror that his face was as white as chalk. For the first time he had looked Truth in the eyes. Others had lied to him; he had dissembled with himself. He was a drunkard, and had not known it. What he had fondly imagined was a pleasant exhilaration had been maudlin intoxication. His fancied wit had been drivel; his gay humors nothing but the noisy vagaries of a sot. But, never again!

" A glass of seltzer," he said to the bartender.

A little silence fell upon the group of his cronies, who had been expecting him to join them.

" Going off the stuff, Bob? " one of them asked politely and with more formality than the highballs ever called forth.

" Yes," said Babbitt.

Some one of the group took up the unwashed thread of a story he had been telling; the bartender shoved over a dime and a nickel change from the quarter, ungarnished with his customary smile; and Babbitt walked out.

Now, Babbitt had a home and a wife — but that is another story. And I will tell you that story, which will show you a better habit and a worse story than you could find in the man who invented the phrase.

It began away up in Sullivan County, where so many rivers and so much trouble begins — or begin; how would you say that? It was July, and Jessie was a summer boarder at the Mountain Squint Hotel, and Bob, who was just out of college, saw her one day — and they were married in September. That's the tabloid novel — one swallow of water, and it's gone.

But those July days!

Let the exclamation point expound it, for I shall not. For particulars you might read up on " Romeo and Juliet," and Abraham Lincoln's thrilling sonnet about " You can fool some of the people," &c., and Darwin's works.

But one thing I must tell you about. Both of them were mad over Omar's Rubaiyat. They knew every verse of the old bluffer by heart — not consecutively, but picking 'em out here and there as you fork the mushrooms in a fifty-cent steak à la Bordelaise. Sullivan County is full of rocks and trees; and Jessie used to sit on them, and — please be good — used to sit on the rocks; and Bob had a way of standing behind her with his hands over her shoulders holding her hands, and his face close to hers, and they would repeat over and over their favorite verses of the old tent-maker. They saw only the poetry and philosophy of the lines then — indeed, they agreed that the Wine was only an image, and that what was meant to be celebrated was some divinity, or maybe Love or Life. However, at that time neither of them had tasted the stuff that goes with a sixty-cent *table d'hote*.

Where was I? Oh, they married and came to New York. Bob showed his college diploma, and accepted a position filling inkstands in a lawyer's office at $15 a week. At the end of two years he had worked up to $50, and gotten his first taste of Bohemia — the kind that won't stand the borax and formaldehyde tests.

They had two furnished rooms and a little kitchen. To Jess, accustomed to the mild but beautiful savor of a country town, the dreggy Bohemia was sugar and spice. She hung fish seines on the walls of her rooms, and bought a rakish-looking sideboard, and learned to play the banjo. Twice or thrice a week they dined at French or Italian *tables d'hote* in a cloud of smoke, and brag and unshorn hair. Jess learned to drink a cocktail in order to get the cherry. At home she smoked a cigarette after dinner. She learned to pronounce Chianti, and leave her olive stones for the waiter to pick up. Once she esayed to say la, la, la! in a crowd but got only as far as the second one. They met one or two couples while dining out and became friendly with them. The sideboard was stocked with Scotch and rye and a liqueur. They had their new friends in to dinner and all were laughing at nothing by 1 A. M. Some plastering fell in the

room below them, for which Bob had to pay $4.50.
Thus they footed it merrily on the ragged frontiers of
the country that has no boundary lines or government.

And soon Bob fell in with his cronies and learned
to keep his foot on the little rail six inches above the
floor for an hour or so every afternoon before he
went home.   Drink always rubbed him the right way,
and he would reach his rooms as jolly as a sandboy.
Jessie would meet him at the door, and generally they
would dance some insane kind of a rigadoon about the
floor by way of greeting.   Once when Bob's feet
became confused and he tumbled headlong over a
foot-stool Jessie laughed so heartily and long that he
had to throw all the couch pillows at her to make her
hush.

In such wise life was speeding for them on the day
when Bob Babbitt first felt the power that the giftie
gi'ed him.

But let us get back to our lamb and mint sauce.

When Bob got home that evening he found Jessie
in a long apron cutting up a lobster for the Newburg.
Usually when Bob came in mellow from his hour at
the bar his welcome was hilarious, though somewhat
tinctured with Scotch smoke.

By screams and snatches of song and certain audible
testimonials of domestic felicity was his advent pro-
claimed.   When she heard his foot on the stairs the
old maid in the hall room always stuffed cotton into

her ears. At first Jessie had shrunk from the rude-
ness and flavor of these spiritual greetings, but as the
fog of the false Bohemia gradually encompassed her
she came to accept them as love's true and proper
greeting.

Bob came in without a word, smiled, kissed her
neatly but noiselessly, took up a paper and sat down.
In the hall room the old maid held her two plugs of
cotton poised, filled with anxiety.

Jessie dropped lobster and knife and ran to him
with frightened eyes.

" What's the matter, Bob, are you ill? "

" Not at all, dear."

" Then what's the matter with you? "

" Nothing."

Hearken, brethren. When She-who-has-a-right-to-
ask interrogates you concerning a change she finds in
your mood answer her thus: Tell her that you, in a
sudden rage, have murdered your grandmother; tell
her that you have robbed orphans and that remorse
has stricken you; tell her your fortune is swept away;
that you are beset by enemies, by bunions, by any kind
of malevolent fate; but do not, if peace and happiness
are worth as much as a grain of mustard seed to you
— do not answer her " Nothing."

Jessie went back to the lobster in silence. She cast
looks of darkest suspicion at Bob. He had never
acted that way before.

When dinner was on the table she set out the bottle of Scotch and the glasses. Bob declined.

" Tell you the truth, Jess," he said. " I've cut out the drink. Help yourself, of course. If you don't mind I'll try some of the seltzer straight."

" You've stopped drinking? " she said, looking at him steadily and unsmilingly. " What for? "

" It wasn't doing me any good," said Bob. " Don't you approve of the idea? "

Jessie raised her eyebrows and one shoulder slightly.

" Entirely," she said with a sculptured smile. " I could not conscientiously advise any one to drink or smoke, or whistle on Sunday."

The meal was finished almost in silence. Bob tried to make talk, but his efforts lacked the stimulus of previous evenings. He felt miserable, and once or twice his eye wandered toward the bottle, but each time the scathing words of his bibulous friend sounded in his ear, and his mouth set with determination.

Jessie felt the change deeply. The essence of their lives seemed to have departed suddenly. The restless fever, the false gayety, the unnatural excitement of the shoddy Bohemia in which they had lived had dropped away in the space of the popping of a cork. She stole curious and forlorn glances at the dejected Bob, who bore the guilty look of at least a wife-beater or a family tyrant.

After dinner the colored maid who came in daily

64

to perform such chores cleared away the things. Jessie, with an unreadable countenance, brought back the bottle of Scotch and the glasses and a bowl of cracked ice and set them on the table.

" May I ask," she said, with some of the ice in her tones, " whether I am to be included in your sudden spasm of goodness? If not, I'll make one for myself. It's rather chilly this evening, for some reason."

" Oh, come now, Jess," said Bob good-naturedly, " don't be too rough on me. Help yourself, by all means. There's no danger of your overdoing it. But I thought there was with me; and that's why I quit. Have yours, and then let's get out the banjo and try over that new quickstep."

" I've heard," said Jessie in the tones of the oracle, " that drinking alone is a pernicious habit. No, I don't think I feel like playing this evening. If we are going to reform we may as well abandon the evil habit of banjo-playing, too."

She took up a book and sat in her little willow rocker on the other side of the table. Neither of them spoke for half an hour.

And then Bob laid down his paper and got up with a strange, absent look on his face and went behind her chair and reached over her shoulders, taking her hands in his, and laid his face close to hers.

In a moment to Jessie the walls of the seine-hung room vanished, and she saw the Sullivan County hills

and rills.   Bob felt her hands quiver in his as he began the verse from old Omar:

" Come, fill the Cup, and in the Fire of Spring
   The Winter Garment of Repentance fling:
   The Bird of Time has but a little way
   To fly — and Lo! the Bird is on the Wing! "

And then he walked to the table and poured a stiff
drink of Scotch into a glass.

But in that moment a mountain breeze had somehow found its way in and blown away the mist of the
false Bohemia.

Jessie leaped and with one fierce sweep of her hand
sent the bottle and glasses crashing to the floor.   The
same motion of her arm carried it around Bob's neck,
where it met its mate and fastened tight.

" Oh, my God, Bobbie — not that verse — I see
now.   I wasn't always such a fool, was I?   The other
one, boy — the one that says: ' Remould it to the
Heart's Desire.'   Say that one —' to the Heart's
Desire.' "

" I know that one," said Bob.   " It goes:

" ' Ah! Love, could you and I with Him conspire
   To grasp this sorry Scheme of Things entire
   Would not we —' "

" Let me finish it," said Jessie.

" ' Would not we shatter it to bits — and then
   Remould it nearer to the Heart's Desire!' "

"*Jessie leaped and with one fierce sweep of her hand sent the bottle and glasses crashing to the floor.*"

" It's shattered all right," said Bob, crunching some glass under his heel.

In some dungeon below the accurate ear of Mrs. Pickens, the landlady, located the smash.

" It's that wild Mr. Babbitt coming home soused again," she said.   " And he's got such a nice little wife, too! "

THE BUYER FROM CACTUS CITY

IT is well that hay fever and colds do not obtain in
the healthful vicinity of Cactus City, Texas, for
the dry goods emporium of Navarro & Platt, situated
there, is not to be sneezed at.

Twenty thousand people in Cactus City scatter
their silver coin with liberal hands for the things that
their hearts desire. The bulk of this semiprecious
metal goes to Navarro & Platt. Their huge brick
building covers enough ground to graze a dozen head
of sheep. You can buy of them a rattlesnake-skin
necktie, an automobile or an eighty-five dollar, latest
style, ladies' tan coat in twenty different shades.
Navarro & Platt first introduced pennies west of the
Colorado River. They had been ranchmen with business heads, who saw that the world did not necessarily
have to cease its revolutions after free grass went out.

Every spring, Navarro, senior partner, fifty-five,
half Spanish, cosmopolitan, able, polished, had " gone
on " to New York to buy goods. This year he shied
at taking up the long trail. He was undoubtedly
growing older; and he looked at his watch several
times a day before the hour came for his siesta.

" John," he said, to his junior partner, " you shall go on this year to buy the goods."

Platt looked tired.

" I'm told," said he, " that New York is a plumb dead town; but I'll go. I can take a whirl in San Antone for a few days on my way and have some fun."

Two weeks later a man in a Texas full dress suit — black frock coat, broad-brimmed soft white hat, and lay-down collar 3-4 inch high, with black, wrought iron necktie — entered the wholesale cloak and suit establishment of Zizzbaum & Son, on lower Broadway.

Old Zizzbaum had the eye of an osprey, the memory of an elephant and a mind that unfolded from him in three movements like the puzzle of the carpenter's rule. He rolled to the front like a brunette polar bear, and shook Platt's hand.

" And how is the good Mr. Navarro in Texas? " he said. " The trip was too long for him this year, so? We welcome Mr. Platt instead."

" A bull's eye," said Platt, " and I'd give forty acres of unirrigated Pecos County land to know how you did it."

" I knew," grinned Zizzbaum, " just as I know that the rainfall in El Paso for the year was 28.5 inches, or an increase of 15 inches, and that therefore Navarro & Platt will buy a $15,000 stock of suits this spring instead of $10,000, as in a dry year. But that will be to-morrow. There is first a cigar in my private office that will remove from your mouth the taste of the ones you smuggle across the Rio Grande and like — because they are smuggled."

It was late in the afternoon and business for the day had ended, Zizzbaum left Platt with a half-smoked cigar, and came out of the private office to Son, who was arranging his diamond scarfpin before a mirror, ready to leave.

" Abey," he said, " you will have to take Mr. Platt around to-night and show him things. They are customers for ten years. Mr. Navarro and I we played chess every moment of spare time when he came. That is good, but Mr. Platt is a young man and this is his first visit to New York. He should amuse easily."

" All right," said Abey, screwing the guard tightly on his pin. " I'll take him on. After he's seen the Flatiron and the head waiter at the Hotel Astor and heard the phonograph play 'Under the Old Apple Tree' it'll be half past ten, and Mr. Texas will be ready to roll up in his blanket. I've got a supper engagement at 11.30, but he'll be all to the Mrs. Winslow before then."

The next morning at 10 Platt walked into the store ready to do business. He had a bunch of hyacinths pinned on his lapel. Zizzbaum himself waited on him

Navarro & Platt were good customers, and never failed to take their discount for cash.

"And what did you think of our little town?" asked Zizzbaum, with the fatuous smile of the Manhattanite.

"I shouldn't care to live in it," said the Texan. "Your son and I knocked around quite a little last night. You've got good water, but Cactus City is better lit up."

"We've got a few lights on Broadway, don't you think, Mr. Platt?"

"And a good many shadows," said Platt. "I think I like your horses best. I haven't seen a crowbait since I've been in town."

Zizzbaum led him upstairs to show the samples of suits.

"Ask Miss Asher to come," he said to a clerk.

Miss Asher came, and Platt, of Navarro & Platt, felt for the first time the wonderful bright light of romance and glory descend upon him. He stood still as a granite cliff above the cañon of the Colorado, with his wide-open eyes fixed upon her. She noticed his look and flushed a little, which was contrary to her custom.

Miss Asher was the crack model of Zizzbaum & Son. She was of the blond type known as "medium," and her measurements even went the required 38-25-42 standard a little better. She had been at Zizzbaum's

two years, and knew her business. Her eye was
bright, but cool; and had she chosen to match her gaze
against the optic of the famed basilisk, that fabulous
monster's gaze would have wavered and softened first.
Incidentally, she knew buyers.

"Now, Mr. Platt," said Zizzbaum, "I want you to
see these princess gowns in the light shades. They
will be the thing in your climate. This first, if you
please, Miss Asher."

Swiftly in and out of the dressing-room the prize
model flew, each time wearing a new costume and looking more stunning with every change. She posed
with absolute self-possession before the stricken buyer,
who stood, tongue-tied and motionless, while Zizzbaum
orated oilily of the styles. On the model's face was
her faint, impersonal professional smile that seemed
to cover something like weariness or contempt.

When the display was over Platt seemed to hesi-
tate. Zizzbaum was a little anxious, thinking that
his customer might be inclined to try elsewhere. But
Platt was only looking over in his mind the best building sites in Cactus City, trying to select one on which
to build a house for his wife-to-be — who was just
then in the dressing-room taking off an evening gown
of lavender and tulle.

"Take your time, Mr. Platt," said Zizzbaum.
"Think it over to-night. You won't find anybody
else meet our prices on goods like these. I'm afraid

you're having a dull time in New York, Mr. Platt. A young man like you — of course, you miss the society of the ladies. Wouldn't you like a nice young lady to take out to dinner this evening? Miss Asher, now, is a very nice young lady; she will make it agreeable for you."

"Why, she doesn't know me," said Platt, wonderingly. "She doesn't know anything about me. Would she go? I'm not acquainted with her."

"Would she go?" repeated Zizzbaum, with uplifted eyebrows. "Sure, she would go. I will introduce you. Sure, she would go."

He called Miss Asher loudly.

She came, calm and slightly contemptuous, in her white shirt waist and plain black skirt.

"Mr. Platt would like the pleasure of your company to dinner this evening," said Zizzbaum, walking away.

"Sure," said Miss Asher, looking at the ceiling. "I'd be much pleased. Nine-eleven West Twentieth street. What time?"

"Say seven o'clock."

"All right, but please don't come ahead of time. I room with a school teacher, and she doesn't allow any gentlemen to call in the room. There isn't any parlor, so you'll have to wait in the hall. I'll be ready."

At half past seven Platt and Miss Asher sat at a

table in a Broadway restaurant. She was dressed in a plain, filmy black. Platt didn't know that it was all a part of her day's work.

With the unobtrusive aid of a good waiter he managed to order a respectable dinner, minus the usual Broadway preliminaries.

Miss Asher flashed upon him a dazzling smile.

" Mayn't I have something to drink? " she asked.

" Why, certainly," said Platt. " Anything you want."

" A dry Martini," she said to the waiter.

When it was brought and set before her Platt reached over and took it away.

" What is this? " he asked.

" A cocktail, of course."

" I thought it was some kind of tea you ordered. This is liquor. You can't drink this. What is your first name? "

" To my intimate friends," said Miss Asher, freezingly, " it is ' Helen.' "

" Listen, Helen," said Platt, leaning over the table. " For many years every time the spring flowers blossomed out on the prairies I got to thinking of somebody that I'd never seen or heard of. I knew it was you the minute I saw you yesterday. I'm going back home to-morrow, and you're going with me. I know it, for I saw it in your eyes when you first looked at me. You needn't kick, for you've got to fall into line.   Here's a little trick I picked out for you on my way over."

He flicked a two-carat diamond solitaire ring across the table.   Miss Asher flipped it back to him with her fork.

" Don't get fresh," she said, severely.

" I'm worth a hundred thousand dollars," said Platt.   " I'll build you the finest house in West Texas."

" You can't buy me, Mr. Buyer," said Miss Asher, " if you had a hundred million.   I didn't think I'd have to call you down.   You didn't look like the others to me at first, but I see you're all alike."

" All who? " asked Platt.

" All you buyers.   You think because we girls have to go out to dinner with you or lose our jobs that you're privileged to say what you please.   Well, forget it.   I thought you were different from the others, but I see I was mistaken."

Platt struck his fingers on the table with a gesture of sudden, illuminating satisfaction.

" I've got it! " he exclaimed, almost hilariously — " the Nicholson place, over on the north side.   There's a big grove of live oaks and a natural lake.   The old house can be pulled down and the new one set further back."

" Put out your pipe," said Miss Asher.   " I'm sorry to wake you up, but you fellows might as well get wise, once for all, to where you stand. I'm supposed to go to dinner with you and help jolly you along so you'll trade with old Zizzy, but don't expect to find me in any of the suits you buy."

" Do you mean to tell me," said Platt, " that you go out this way with customers, and they all — they all talk to you like I have? "

" They all make plays," said Miss Asher. " But I must say that you've got 'em beat in one respect. They generally talk diamonds, while you've actually dug one up."

" How long have you been working, Helen? "

" Got my name pat, haven't you? I've been supporting myself for eight years. I was a cash girl and a wrapper and then a shop girl until I was grown, and then I got to be a suit model. Mr. Texas Man, don't you think a little wine would make this dinner a little less dry? "

" You're not going to drink wine any more, dear. It's awful to think how —— I'll come to the store to-morrow and get you. I want you to pick out an automobile before we leave. That's all we need to buy here."

" Oh, cut that out. If you knew how sick I am of hearing such talk."

After the dinner they walked down Broadway and came upon Diana's little wooded park. The trees caught Platt's eye at once, and he must turn along

"I don't care," said Miss Asher blithely. "I'm going there tomorrow."

under the winding walk beneath them. The lights shone upon two bright tears in the model's eyes.

" I don't like that," said Platt. " What's the matter? "

" Don't you mind," said Miss Asher. " Well, it's because — well, I didn't think you were that kind when I first saw you. But you are all like. And now will you take me home, or will I have to call a cop? "

Platt took her to the door of her boarding-house. They stood for a minute in the vestibule. She looked at him with such scorn in her eyes that even his heart of oak began to waver. His arm was half way around her waist, when she struck him a stinging blow on the face with her open hand.

As he stepped back a ring fell from somewhere and bounded on the tiled floor. Platt groped for it and found it.

" Now, take your useless diamond and go, Mr. Buyer," she said.

" This was the other one — the wedding ring," said the Texan, holding the smooth gold band on the palm of his hand.

Miss Asher's eyes blazed upon him in the half darkness.

" Was that what you meant? — did you " —

Somebody opened the door from inside the house.

" Good-night," said Platt. " I'll see you at the store to-morrow."

Miss Asher ran up to her room and shook the school teacher until she sat up in bed ready to scream " Fire! "

" Where is it? " she cried.

" That's what I want to know," said the model. " You've studied geography, Emma, and you ought to know. Where is a town called Cac — Cac — Carac — Caracas City, I think they called it? "

" How dare you wake me up for that? " said the school teacher. " Caracas is in Venezuela, of course."

" What's it like? "

" Why, it's principally earthquakes and negroes and monkeys and malarial fever and volcanoes."

" I don't care," said Miss Asher, blithely; " I'm going there to-morrow."

THE BADGE OF POLICEMAN O'ROON

IT cannot be denied that men and women have looked upon one another for the first time and become instantly enamored. It is a risky process, this love at first sight, before she has seen him in Bradstreet or he has seen her in curl papers. But these things do happen; and one instance must form a theme for this story — though not, thank Heaven, to the overshadowing of more vital and important subjects, such as drink, policemen, horses and earldoms.

During a certain war a troop calling itself the Gentle Riders rode into history and one or two ambuscades. The Gentle Riders were recruited from the aristocracy of the wild men of the West and the wild men of the aristocracy of the East. In khaki there is little telling them one from another, so they became good friends and comrades all around.

Ellsworth Remsen, whose old Knickerbocker descent atoned for his modest rating at only ten millions, ate his canned beef gayly by the campfires of the Gentle Riders. The war was a great lark to him, so that he scarcely regretted polo and planked shad.

One of the troopers was a well set up, affable, cool

young man, who called himself O'Roon. To this
young man Remsen took an especial liking. The two
rode side by side during the famous mooted up-hill
charge that was disputed so hotly at the time by the
Spaniards and afterward by the Democrats.

After the war Remsen came back to his polo and
shad. One day a well set up, affable, cool young man
disturbed him at his club, and he and O'Roon were
soon pounding each other and exchanging opprobrious
epithets after the manner of long-lost friends.
O'Roon looked seedy and out of luck and perfectly
contented. But it seemed that his content was only
apparent.

" Get me a job, Remsen," he said. " I've just
handed a barber my last shilling."

" No trouble at all," said Remsen. " I know a lot
of men who have banks and stores and things downtown. Any particular line you fancy? "

" Yes," said O'Roon, with a look of interest. " I
took a walk in your Central Park this morning. I'd
like to be one of those bobbies on horseback. That
would be about the ticket. Besides, it's the only thing
I could do. I can ride a little and the fresh air suits
me. Think you could land that for me? "

Remsen was sure that he could. And in a very
short time he did. And they who were not above looking at mounted policemen might have seen a well set
up, affable, cool young man on a prancing chestnut

steed attending to his duties along the driveways of
the park.

And now at the extreme risk of wearying old gentlemen who carry leather fob chains, and elderly
ladies who — but no! grandmother herself yet thrills
at foolish, immortal Romeo — there must be a hint of
love at first sight.

It came just as Remsen was strolling into Fifth
avenue from his club a few doors away.

A motor car was creeping along foot by foot, im-
peded by a freshet of vehicles that filled the street.
In the car was a chauffeur and an old gentleman with
snowy side whiskers and a Scotch plaid cap which
could not be worn while automobiling except by a personage. Not even a wine agent would dare to do it.
But these two were of no consequence — except, perhaps, for the guiding of the machine and the paying
for it. At the old gentleman's side sat a young lady
more beautiful than pomegranate blossoms, more ex-
quisite than the first quarter moon viewed at twilight
through the tops of oleanders. Remsen saw her and
knew his fate. He could have flung himself under
the very wheels that conveyed her, but he knew that
would be the last means of attracting the attention
of those who ride in motor cars. Slowly the auto
passed, and, if we place the poets above the autoists,
carried the heart of Remsen with it. Here was a
large city of millions, and many women who at

certain distance appear to resemble pomegranate blossoms. Yet he hoped to see her again; for each one fancies that his romance has its own tutelary guardian and divinity.

Luckily for Remsen's peace of mind there came a diversion in the guise of a reunion of the Gentle Riders of the city. There were not many of them — perhaps a score — and there was wassail, and things to eat, and speeches and the Spaniard was bearded again in recapitulation. And when daylight threatened them the survivors prepared to depart. But some remained upon the battlefield. One of these was Trooper O'Roon, who was not seasoned to potent liquids. His legs declined to fulfil the obligations they had sworn to the police department.

" I'm stewed, Remsen," said O'Roon to his friend. " Why do they built hotels that go round and round like catherine wheels? They'll take away my shield and break me. I can think and talk con-con-consec-sec-secutively, but I s-s-stammer with my feet. I've got to go on duty in three hours. The jig is up, Remsen. The jig is up, I tell you."

" Look at me," said Remsen, who was his smiling self, pointing to his own face; " whom do you see here? "

" Goo' fellow," said O'Roon, dizzily, " Goo' old Remsen."

" Not so," said Remsen. " You see Mounted Policeman O'Roon. Look at your face — no; you can't do that without a glass — but look at mine, and think of yours. How much alike are we? As two French *table d'hote* dinners. With your badge, on your horse, in your uniform, will I charm nurse-maids and prevent the grass from growing under people's feet in the Park this day. I will save your badge and your honor, besides having the jolliest lark I've been blessed with since we licked Spain.

Promptly on time the counterfeit presentment of Mounted Policeman O'Roon single-footed into the Park on his chestnut steed. In a uniform two men who are unlike will look alike; two who somewhat resemble each other in feature and figure will appear as twin brothers. So Remsen trotted down the bridle paths, enjoying himself hugely, so few real pleasures do ten-millionaires have.

Along the driveway in the early morning spun a victoria drawn by a pair of fiery bays. There was something foreign about the affair, for the Park is rarely used in the morning except by unimportant people who love to be healthy, poor and wise. In the vehicle sat an old gentleman with snowy side-whiskers and a Scotch plaid cap which could not be worn while driving except by a personage. At his side sat the lady of Remsen's heart — the lady who looked like pomegranate blossoms and the gibbous moon.

Remsen met them coming. At the instant of their

passing her eyes looked into his, and but for the ever coward heart of a true lover he could have sworn that she flushed a faint pink. He trotted on for twenty yards, and then wheeled his horse at the sound of runaway hoofs. The bays had bolted.

Remsen sent his chestnut after the victoria like a shot. There was work cut out for the impersonator of Policeman O'Roon. The chestnut ranged alongside the off bay thirty seconds after the chase began, rolled his eye back at Remsen, and said in the only manner open to policemen's horses:

" Well, you duffer, are you going to do your share? You're not O'Roon, but it seems to me if you'd lean to the right you could reach the reins of that foolish, slow-running bay — ah! you're all right; O'Roon couldn't have done it more neatly! "

The runaway team was tugged to an inglorious halt by Remsen's tough muscles. The driver released his hands from the wrapped reins, jumped from his seat and stood at the heads of the team. The chestnut, approving his new rider, danced and pranced, reviling equinely the subdued bays. Remsen, lingering, was dimly conscious of a vague, impossible, unnecessary old gentleman in a Scotch cap who talked incessantly about something. And he was acutely conscious of a pair of violet eyes that would have drawn Saint Pyrites from his iron pillar — or whatever the allusion is — and of the lady's smile and look — a little frightened, but a look that, with the ever coward heart of a true lover, he could not yet construe. They were asking his name and bestowing upon him well-bred thanks for his heroic deed, and the Scotch cap was especially babbling and insistent. But the eloquent appeal was in the eyes of the lady.

A little thrill of satisfaction ran through Remsen, because he had a name to give which, without undue pride, was worthy of being spoken in high places, and a small fortune which, with due pride, he could leave at his end without disgrace.

He opened his lips to speak, and closed them again. Who was he? Mounted Policeman O'Roon. The badge and the honor of his comrade were in his hands. If Ellsworth Remsen, ten-millionaire and Knickerbocker, had just rescued pomegranate blossoms and Scotch cap from possible death, where was Policeman O'Roon? Off his beat, exposed, disgraced, discharged. Love had come, but before that there had been something that demanded precedence — the fellowship of men on battlefields fighting an alien foe.

Remsen touched his cap, looked between the chestnut's ears, and took refuge in vernacularity.

"Don't mention it," he said stolidly. "We policemen are paid to do these things. It's our duty."

And he rode away — rode away cursing *noblesse oblige*, but knowing he could never have done anything else.

At the end of the day Remsen sent the chestnut to his stable and went to O'Roon's room. The policeman was again a well set up, affable, cool young man who sat by the window smoking cigars.

" I wish you and the rest of the police force and all badges, horses, brass buttons and men who can't drink two glasses of *brut* without getting upset were at the devil," said Remsen feelingly.

O'Roon smiled with evident satisfaction.

" Good old Remsen," he said, affably, " I know all about it. They trailed me down and cornered me here two hours ago. There was a little row at home, you know, and I cut sticks just to show them. I don't believe I told you that my Governor was the Earl of Ardsley. Funny you should bob against them in the Park. If you damaged that horse of mine I'll never forgive you. I'm going to buy him and take him back with me. Oh, yes, and I think my sister — Lady Angela, you know — wants particularly for you to come up to the hotel with me this evening. Didn't lose my badge, did you, Remsen? I've got to turn that in at Headquarters when I resign."

THE LAST LEAF

IN a little district west of Washington Square the streets have run crazy and broken themselves into small strips called " places." These " places " make strange angles and curves. One street crosses itself a time or two. An artist once discovered a valuable possibility in this street. Suppose a collector with a bill for paints, paper and canvas should, in traversing this route, suddenly meet himself coming back, without a cent having been paid on account!

So, to quaint old Greenwich Village the art people soon came prowling, hunting for north windows and eighteenth-century gables and Dutch attics and low rents. Then they imported some pewter mugs and a chafing dish or two from Sixth avenue, and became a " colony."

At the top of a squatty, three-story brick Sue and Johnsy had their studio. " Johnsy " was familiar for Joanna. One was from Maine; the other from California. They had met at the *table d'hote* of an Eighth street " Delmonico's," and found their tastes in art, chicory salad and bishop sleeves so congenial that the joint studio resulted.

That was in May. In November a cold, unseen stranger, whom the doctors called Pneumonia, stalked about the colony, touching one here and there with his icy fingers. Over on the east side this ravager strode boldly, smiting his victims by scores, but his feet trod slowly through the maze of the narrow and moss-grown " places."

Mr. Pneumonia was not what you would call a chivalric old gentleman. A mite of a little woman with blood thinned by California zephyrs was hardly fair game for the red-fisted, short-breathed old duffer. But Johnsy he smote; and she lay, scarcely moving, on her painted iron bedstead, looking through the small Dutch window-panes at the blank side of the next brick house.

One morning the busy doctor invited Sue into the hallway with a shaggy, gray eyebrow.

" She has one chance in — let us say, ten," he said; as he shook down the mercury in his clinical thermometer. " And that chance is for her to want to live. This way people have of lining-up on the side of the undertaker makes the entire pharmacopeia look silly. Your little lady has made up her mind that she's not going to get well. Has she anything on her mind? "

" She — she wanted to paint the Bay of Naples some day," said Sue.

" Paint? — bosh! Has she anything on her mind

worth thinking about twice — a man, for instance? "

" A man? " said Sue, with a jew's-harp twang in
her voice. " Is a man worth — but, no, doctor; there
is nothing of the kind.

" Well, it is the weakness, then," said the doctor.
" I will do all that science, so far as it may filter
through my efforts, can accomplish. But whenever
my patient begins to count the carriages in her funeral procession I subtract 50 per cent. from the cura-
tive power of medicines. If you will get her to ask
one question about the new winter styles in cloak
sleeves I will promise you a one-in-five chance for her,
instead of one in ten."

After the doctor had gone Sue went into the work-
room and cried a Japanese napkin to a pulp. Then
she swaggered into Johnsy's room with her drawing
board, whistling ragtime.

Johnsy lay, scarcely making a ripple under the
bedclothes, with her face toward the window. Sue
stopped whistling, thinking she was asleep.

She arranged her board and began a pen-and-ink
drawing to illustrate a magazine story. Young
artists must pave their way to Art by drawing pictures for magazine stories that young authors write
to pave their way to Literature.

As Sue was sketching a pair of elegant horse-
show riding trousers and a monocle on the figure of
the hero, an Idaho cowboy, she heard a low sound,

several times repeated. She went quickly to the bedside.

Johnsy's eyes were open wide. She was looking out the window and counting — counting backward.

"Twelve," she said, and a little later "eleven;" and then "ten," and "nine;" and then "eight" and "seven," almost together.

Sue looked solicitously out the window. What was there to count? There was only a bare, dreary yard to be seen, and the blank side of the brick house twenty feet away. An old, old ivy vine, gnarled and decayed at the roots, climbed half way up the brick wall. The cold breath of autumn had stricken its leaves from the vine until its skeleton branches clung, almost bare, to the crumbling bricks.

"What is it, dear?" asked Sue.

"Six," said Johnsy, in almost a whisper. "They're falling faster now. Three days ago there were almost a hundred. It made my head ache to count them. But now it's easy. There goes another one. There are only five left now."

"Five what, dear. Tell your Sudie."

"Leaves. On the ivy vine. When the last one falls I must go, too. I've known that for three days. Didn't the doctor tell you?"

"Oh, I never heard of such nonsense," complained Sue, with magnificent scorn. "What have old ivy leaves to do with your getting well? And you used to love that vine so, you naughty girl. Don't be a goosey. Why, the doctor told me this morning that your chances for getting well real soon were — let's see exactly what he said — he said the chances were ten to one! Why, that's almost as good a chance as we have in New York when we ride on the street cars or walk past a new building. Try to take some broth now, and let Sudie go back to her drawing, so she can sell the editor man with it, and buy port wine for her sick child, and pork chops for her greedy self."

"You needn't get any more wine," said Johnsy, keeping her eyes fixed out the window. "There goes another. No, I don't want any broth. That leaves just four. I want to see the last one fall before it gets dark. Then I'll go, too."

"Johnsy, dear," said Sue, bending over her, "will you promise me to keep your eyes closed, and not look out the window until I am done working? I must hand those drawings in by to-morrow. I need the light, or I would draw the shade down."

"Couldn't you draw in the other room?" asked Johnsy, coldly.

"I'd rather be here by you," said Sue. "Besides, I don't want you to keep looking at those silly ivy leaves."

"Tell me as soon as you have finished," said Johnsy, closing her eyes, and lying white and still as a fallen statue, " because I want to see the last one fall. I'm tired of waiting. I'm tired of thinking. I went to turn loose my hold on everything, and go sailing down, down, just like one of those poor, tired leaves."

" Try to sleep," said Sue. " I must call Behrman up to be my model for the old hermit miner. I'll not be gone a minute. Don't try to move 'till I come back."

Old Behrman was a painter who lived on the ground floor beneath them. He was past sixty and had a Michael Angelo's Moses beard curling down from the head of a satyr along the body of an imp. Behrman was a failure in art. Forty years he had wielded the brush without getting near enough to touch the hem of his Mistress's robe. He had been always about to paint a masterpiece, but had never yet begun it. For several years he had painted nothing except now and then a daub in the line of commerce or advertising. He earned a little by serving as a model to those young artists in the colony who could not pay the price of a professional. He drank gin to excess, and still talked of his coming masterpiece. For the rest he was a fierce little old man, who scoffed terribly at softness in any one, and who regarded himself as especial mastiff-in-waiting to protect the two young artists in the studio above.

Sue found Behrman smelling strongly of juniper

berries in his dimly lighted den below. In one corner was a blank canvas on an easel that had been waiting there for twenty-five years to receive the first line of the masterpiece. She told him of Johnsy's fancy, and how she feared she would, indeed, light and fragile as a leaf herself, float away when her slight hold upon the world grew weaker.

Old Behrman, with his red eyes plainly streaming, shouted his contempt and derision for such idiotic imaginings.

"Vass!" he cried. "Is dere people in de world mit der foolishness to die because leafs dey drop off from a confounded vine? I haf not heard of such a thing. No, I vill not bose as a model for your fool hermit-dunderhead. Vy do you allow dot silly pusiness to come in der prain of her? Ach, dot poor lettle Miss Johnsy."

"She is very ill and weak," said Sue, "and the fever has left her mind morbid and full of strange fancies. Very well, Mr. Behrman, if you do not care to pose for me, you needn't. But I think you are a horrid old — old flibbertigibbet."

"You are just like a woman!" yelled Behrman. "Who said I vill not bose? Go on. I come mit you. For half an hour I haf peen trying to say dot I am ready to bose. Gott! dis is not any blace in which one so goot as Miss Yohnsy shall lie sick.

Some day I vill baint a masterpiece, and ve shall all
go avay. Gott! yes."

Johnsy was sleeping when they went upstairs. Sue
pulled the shade down to the window-sill, and mo-
tioned Behrman into the other room. In there they
peered out the window fearfully at the ivy vine.
Then they looked at each other for a moment without speaking. A persistent, cold rain was falling,
mingled with snow. Behrman, in his old blue shirt,
took his seat as the hermit-miner on an upturned
kettle for a rock.

When Sue awoke from an hour's sleep the next
morning she found Johnsy with dull, wide-open eyes
staring at the drawn green shade.

"Pull it up; I want to see," she ordered, in a
whisper.

Wearily Sue obeyed.

But, lo! after the beating rain and fierce gusts of
wind that had endured through the livelong night,
there yet stood out against the brick wall one ivy
leaf. It was the last on the vine. Still dark green
near its stem, but with its serrated edges tinted with
the yellow of dissolution and decay, it hung bravely
from a branch some twenty feet above the ground.

"It is the last one," said Johnsy. "I thought it
would surely fall during the night. I heard the wind.
It will fall to-day, and I shall die at the same time."

"But lo! after the beating rain and gusts of wind that had endured through the livelong night, there yet stood out against the brick wall one ivy leaf."

"Dear, dear!" said Sue, leaning her worn face down to the pillow, "think of me, if you won't think of yourself. What would I do?"

But Johnsy did not answer. The lonesomest thing in all the world is a soul when it is making ready to go on its mysterious, far journey. The fancy seemed to possess her more strongly as one by one the ties that bound her to friendship and to earth were loosed.

The day wore away, and even through the twilight they could see the lone ivy leaf clinging to its stem against the wall. And then, with the coming of the night the north wind was again loosed, while the rain still beat against the windows and pattered down from the low Dutch eaves.

When it was light enough Johnsy, the merciless, commanded that the shade be raised.

The ivy leaf was still there.

Johnsy lay for a long time looking at it. And then she called to Sue, who was stirring her chicken broth over the gas stove.

"I've been a bad girl, Sudie," said Johnsy. "Something has made that last leaf stay there to show me how wicked I was. It is a sin to want to die. You may bring me a little broth now, and some milk with a little port in it, and — no; bring me a hand-mirror first, and then pack some pillows about me, and I will sit up and watch you cook."

An hour later she said.

"Sudie, some day I hope to paint the Bay of Naples."

The doctor came in the afternoon, and Sue had an excuse to go into the hallway as he left.

"Even chances," said the doctor, taking Sue's thin, shaking hand in his. "With good nursing you'll win. And now I must see another case I have downstairs. Behrman, his name is — some kind of an artist, I believe. Pneumonia, too. He is an old, weak man, and the attack is acute. There is no hope for him; but he goes to the hospital to-day to be made more comfortable."

The next day the doctor said to Sue: "She's out of danger. You've won. Nutrition and care now — that's all."

And that afternoon Sue came to the bed where Johnsy lay, contentedly knitting a very blue and very useless woolen shoulder scarf, and put one arm around her, pillows and all.

"I have something to tell you, white mouse," she said. "Mr. Behrman died of pneumonia to-day in the hospital. He was ill only two days. The janitor found him on the morning of the first day in his room downstairs helpless with pain. His shoes and clothing were wet through and icy cold. They couldn't imagine where he had been on such a dreadful night. And then they found a lantern, still lighted, and a ladder that had been dragged from its place, and some scattered brushes, and a palette with green and yellow colors mixed on it, and — look out the window, dear, at the last ivy leaf on the wall. Didn't you wonder why it never fluttered or moved when the wind blew? Ah, darling, it's Behrman's masterpiece — he painted it there the night that the last leaf fell."

THE TALE OF A TAINTED TENNER

MONEY talks. But you may think that the conversation of a little old ten-dollar bill in New York would be nothing more than a whisper. Oh, very well! Pass up this *sotto voce* autobiography of an X if you like. If you are one of the kind that prefers to listen to John D.'s checkbook roar at you through a megaphone as it passes by, all right. But don't forget that small change can say a word to the point now and then. The next time you tip your grocer's clerk a silver quarter to give you extra weight of his boss's goods read the four words above the lady's head. How are they for repartee?

I am a ten-dollar Treasury note, series of 1901. You may have seen one in a friend's hand. On my face, in the centre, is a picture of the bison Americanus, miscalled a buffalo by fifty or sixty millions of Americans. The heads of Capt. Lewis and Capt. Clark adorn the ends. On my back is the graceful figure of Liberty or Ceres or Maxine Elliot standing in the centre of the stage on a conservatory plant. My references is — or are — Section 3,588, Revised Statutes. Ten cold, hard dollars — I don't say whether silver, gold, lead or iron — Uncle Sam will hand you over his counter if you want to cash me in.

I beg you will excuse any conversational breaks that I make — thanks, I knew you would — got that sneaking little respect and agreeable feeling toward even an X, haven't you? You see, a tainted bill doesn't have much chance to acquire a correct form of expression. I never knew a really cultured and educated person that could afford to hold a ten-spot any longer than it would take to do an Arthur Duffy to the nearest That's All! sign or delicatessen store.

For a six-year-old, I've had a lively and gorgeous circulation. I guess I've paid as many debts as the man who dies. I've been owned by a good many kinds of people. But a little old ragged, damp, dingy five-dollar silver certificate gave me a jar one day. I was next to it in the fat and bad-smelling purse of a butcher.

"Hey, you Sitting Bull," says I, "don't scrouge so. Anyhow, don't you think it's about time you went in on a customs payment and got reissued? For a series of 1899 you're a sight."

"Oh, don't get crackly just because you're a Buffalo bill," says the fiver. "You'd be limp, too, if you'd been stuffed down in a thick cotton-and-lisle-thread under an elastic all day, and the thermometer not a degree under 85 in the store."

"I never heard of a pocketbook like that," says I. "Who carried you?"

" A shopgirl," says the five-spot.

" What's that? " I had to ask.

" You'll never know till their millennium comes,"
says the fiver.

Just then a two-dollar bill behind me with a George
Washington head, spoke up to the fiver:

" Aw, cut out yer kicks. Ain't lisle thread good
enough for yer? If you was under all cotton like
I've been to-day, and choked up with factory dust till
the lady with the cornucopia on me sneezed half a
dozen times, you'd have some reason to complain."

That was the next day after I arrived in New York.
I came in a $500 package of tens to a Brooklyn bank
from one of its Pennsylvania correspondents — and I
haven't made the acquaintance of any of the five and
two spot's friends' pocketbooks yet. Silk for mine,
every time.

I was lucky money. I kept on the move. Sometimes I changed hands twenty times a day. I saw
the inside of every business; I fought for my owner's
every pleasure. It seemed that on Saturday nights I
never missed being slapped down on a bar. Tens
were always slapped down, while ones and twos were
slid over to the bartenders folded. I got in the habit
of looking for mine, and I managed to soak in a little
straight or some spilled Martini or Manhattan whenever I could. Once I got tied up in a great greasy
roll of bills in a pushcart peddler's jeans. I thought

I never would get in circulation again, for the future department store owner lived on eight cents' worth of dog meat and onions a day. But this peddler got into trouble one day on account of having his cart too near a crossing, and I was rescued. I always will feel grateful to the cop that got me. He changed me at a cigar store near the Bowery that was running a crap game in the back room. So it was the Captain of the precinct, after all, that did me the best turn, when he got his. He blew me for wine the next evening in a Broadway restaurant; and I really felt as glad to get back again as an Astor does when he sees the lights of Charing Cross.

A tainted ten certainly does get action on Broadway. I was alimony once, and got folded in a little dogskin purse among a lot of dimes. They were bragging about the busy times there were in Ossining whenever three girls got hold of one of them during the ice cream season. But it's Slow Moving Vehicles Keep to the Right for the little Bok tips when you think of the way we bison plasters refuse to stick to anything during the rush lobster hour.

The first I ever heard of tainted money was one night when a good thing with a Van to his name threw me over with some other bills to buy a stack of blues.

About midnight a big, easy-going man with a fat face like a monk's and the eye of a janitor with his wages raised took me and a lot of other notes and rolled us into what is termed a " wad " among the money tainters.

" Ticket me for five hundred," said he to the banker, " and look out for everything, Charlie. I'm going out for a stroll in the glen before the moonlight fades from the brow of the cliff. If anybody finds the roof in their way there's $60,000 wrapped in a comic supplement in the upper left-hand corner of the safe. Be bold; everywhere be bold, but be not bowled over. 'Night."

I found myself between two $20 gold certificates. One of 'em says to me:

" Well, old shorthorn, you're in luck to-night. You'll see something of life. Old Jack's going to make the Tenderloin look like a hamburg steak."

" Explain," says I. " I'm used to joints, but I don't care for filet mignon with the kind of sauce you serve."

" 'Xcuse me," said the twenty. " Old Jack is the proprietor of this gambling house. He's going on a whiz to-night because he offered $50,000 to a church and it refused to accept it because they said his money was tainted."

" What is a church? " I asked.

" Oh, I forgot," says the twenty, " that I was talking to a tenner. Of course you don't know. You're too much to put into the contribution basket, and not enough to buy anything at a bazaar. A church is —

a large building in which penwipers and tidies are sold at $20 each."

I don't care much about chinning with gold certificates. There's a streak of yellow in 'em. All is not gold that's quitters.

Old Jack certainly was a gilt-edged sport. When it came his time to loosen up he never referred the waiter to an actuary.

By and by it got around that he was smiting the rock in the wilderness; and all along Broadway things with cold noses and hot gullets fell in on our trail. The third Jungle Book was there waiting for somebody to put covers on it. Old Jack's money may have had a taint to it, but all the same he had orders for his Camembert piling up on him every minute. First his friends rallied round him; and then the fellows that his friends knew by sight; and then a few of his enemies buried the hatchet; and finally he was buying souvenirs for so many Neapolitan fisher maidens and butterfly octettes that the head waiters were 'phoning all over town for Julian Mitchell to please come around and get them into some kind of order.

At last we floated into an uptown café that I knew by heart. When the hod-carriers' union in jackets and aprons saw us coming the chief goal kicker called out: " Six — eleven — forty-two — nineteen — twelve " to his men, and they put on nose guards till it was clear whether we meant Port Arthur or

Portsmouth. But Old Jack wasn't working for the furniture and glass factories that night. He sat down quiet and sang "Ramble" in a half-hearted way. His feelings had been hurt, so the twenty told me, because his offer to the church had been refused.

But the wassail went on; and Brady himself couldn't have hammered the thirst mob into a better imitation of the real penchant for the stuff that you screw out of a bottle with a napkin.

Old Jack paid the twenty above me for a round, leaving me on the outside of his roll. He laid the roll on the table and sent for the proprietor.

"Mike," says he, "here's money that the good people have refused. Will it buy of your wares in the name of the devil? They say it's tainted."

"I will," says Mike, "and I'll put it in the drawer next to the bills that was paid to the parson's daughter for kisses at the church fair to build a new parsonage for the parson's daughter to live in."

At 1 o'clock when the hod-carriers were making ready to close up the front and keep the inside open, a woman slips in the door of the restaurant and comes up to Old Jack's table. You've seen the kind — black shawl, creepy hair, ragged skirt, white face, eyes a cross between Gabriel's and a sick kitten's — the kind of woman that's always on the lookout for an automobile or the mendicancy squad — and she stands there without a word and looks at the money.

Old Jack gets up, peels me off the roll and hands me to her with a bow.

" Madam," says he, just like actors I've heard, " here is a tainted bill. I am a gambler. This bill came to me to-night from a gentleman's son. Where he got it I do not know. If you will do me the favor to accept it, it is yours."

The woman took me with a trembling hand.

" Sir," said she, " I counted thousands of this issue of bills into packages when they were virgin from the presses. I was a clerk in the Treasury Department. There was an official to whom I owed my position. You say they are tainted now. If you only knew — but I won't say any more. Thank you with all my heart, sir — thank you — thank you."

Where do you suppose that woman carried me almost at a run? To a bakery. Away from Old Jack and a sizzling good time to a bakery. And I get changed, and she does a Sheridan-twenty-miles-away with a dozen rolls and a section of jelly cake as big as a turbine water-wheel. Of course I lost sight of her then, for I was snowed up in the bakery, wondering whether I'd get changed at the drug store the next day in an alum deal or paid over to the cement works.

A week afterward I butted up against one of the one-dollar bills the baker had given the woman for change.

" Hallo, E35039669," says I, " weren't you in the change for me in a bakery last Saturday night? "

" Yep," says the solitaire in his free and easy style.

" How did the deal turn out? " I asked.

" She blew E17051431 for milk and round steak," says the one-spot. " She kept me till the rent man came. It was a bum room with a sick kid in it. But you ought to have seen him go for the bread and tincture of formaldehyde. Half-starved, I guess. Then she prayed some. Don't get stuck up, tenner. We one-spots hear ten prayers, where you hear one. She said something about ' who giveth to the poor.' Oh, let's cut out the slum talk. I'm certainly tired of the company that keeps me. I wish I was big enough to move in society with you tainted bills."

" Shut up," says I; " there's no such thing. I know the rest of it. There's a ' lendeth to the Lord ' somewhere in it. Now look on my back and read what you see there."

" This note is a legal tender at its face value for all debts public and private."

" This talk about tainted money makes me tired," says I.

V

THE PIMIENTA PANCAKES

WHILE we were rounding up a bunch of the Tri-
angle-O cattle in the Frio bottoms a projecting branch
of a dead mesquite caught my wooden stirrup and gave
my ankle a wrench that laid me up in camp for a
week.

On the third day of my compulsory idleness I crawled
out near the grub wagon, and reclined helpless under
the conversational fire of Judson Odom, the camp cook.
Jud was a monologist by nature, whom Destiny, with
customary blundering, had set in a profession wherein
he was bereaved, for the greater portion of his time,
of an audience.

Therefore, I was manna in the desert of Jud's ob-
mutescence.

Betimes I was stirred by invalid longings for something to eat that did not come under the caption of
" grub." I had visions of the maternal pantry " deep
as first love, and wild with all regret," and then I asked:
" Jud, can you make pancakes? "

Jud laid down his six-shooter, with which he was pre-
paring to pound an antelope steak, and stood over me
in what I felt to be a menacing attitude. He further
indorsed my impression that his pose was resentful by

fixing upon me with his light blue eyes a look of cold suspicion.

"Say, you," he said, with candid, though not excessive, choler, "did you mean that straight, or was you trying to throw the gaff into me? Some of the boys been telling you about me and that pancake racket?"

"No, Jud," I said, sincerely, "I meant it. It seems to me I'd swap my pony and saddle for a stack of buttered brown pancakes with some first crop, open kettle, New Orleans sweetening. Was there a story about pancakes?"

Jud was mollified at once when he saw that I had not been dealing in allusions. He brought some mysterious bags and tin boxes from the grub wagon and set them in the shade of the hackberry where I lay reclined. I watched him as he began to arrange them leisurely and untie their many strings.

"No, not a story," said Jud, as he worked, "but just the logical disclosures in the case of me and that pink-eyed snoozer from Mired Mule Cañada and Miss Willella Learight. I don't mind telling you.

"I was punching then for old Bill Toomey, on the San Miguel. One day I gets all ensnared up in aspirations for to eat some canned grub that hasn't ever mooed or baaed or grunted or been in peck measures. So, I gets on my bronc and pushes the wind for Uncle Emsley Telfair's store at the Pimienta Crossing on the Nueces.

"About three in the afternoon I throwed my bridle rein over a mesquite limb and walked the last twenty yards into Uncle Emsley's store. I got up on the counter and told Uncle Emsley that the signs pointed to the devastation of the fruit crop of the world. In a minute I had a bag of crackers and a long-handled spoon, with an open can each of apricots and pineapples and cherries and greengages beside of me with Uncle Emsley busy chopping away with the hatchet at the yellow clings. I was feeling like Adam before the apple stampede, and was digging my spurs into the side of the counter and working with my twenty-four-inch spoon when I happened to look out of the window into the yard of Uncle Emsley's house, which was next to the store.

" There was a girl standing there — an imported girl with fixings on — philandering with a croquet maul and amusing herself by watching my style of encouraging the fruit canning industry.

" I slid off the counter and delivered up my shovel to Uncle Emsley.

" ' That's my niece,' says he; ' Miss Willella Learight, down from Palestine on a visit. Do you want that I should make you acquainted? '

" ' The Holy Land,' I says to myself, my thoughts milling some as I tried to run 'em into the corral. ' Why not? There was sure angels in Pales — Why yes, Uncle Emsley,' I says out loud, ' I'd be awful edified to meet Miss Learight."

" So Uncle Emsley took me out in the yard and gave us each other's entitlements.

" I never was shy about women. I never could understand why some men who can break a mustang be-

"I was digging my spurs into the side of the counter...when I happened to look outside."

fore breakfast and shave in the dark, get all left-handed
and full of perspiration and excuses when they see a
bolt of calico draped around what belongs in it. Inside of eight minutes me and Miss Willella was aggra-
vating the croquet balls around as amiable as second
cousins. She gave me a dig about the quantity of
canned fruit I had eaten, and I got back at her, flat-
footed, about how a certain lady named Eve started the
fruit trouble in the first free-grass pasture — 'Over in
Palestine, wasn' it? ' says I, as easy and pat as roping
a one-year-old.

"That was how I acquired cordiality for the prox-
imities of Miss Willella Learight; and the disposition
grew larger as time passed. She was stopping at Pimienta Crossing for her health, which was very good, and
for the climate, which was forty per cent. hotter than
Palestine. I rode over to see her once every week for
a while; and then I figured it out that if I doubled the
number of trips I would see her twice as often.

"One week I slipped in a third trip; and that's where
the pancakes and the pink-eyed snoozer busted into the
game.

"That evening, while I set on the counter with a
peach and two damsons in my mouth, I asked Uncle
Emsley how Miss Willella was.

"'Why,' says Uncle Emsley, 'she's gone riding with
Jackson Bird, the sheep man from over at Mired Mule
Cañada.'

"I swallowed the peach seed and the two damson
seeds. I guess somebody held the counter by the bridle

while I got off; and then I walked out straight ahead till
I butted against the mesquite where my roan was tied.

"'She's gone riding,' I whisper in my bronc's ear,
'with Birdstone Jack, the hired mule from Sheep Man's
Cañada. Did you get that, old Leather-and-Gallops?'

"That bronc of mine wept, in his way. He'd been
raised a cow pony and he didn't care for snoozers.

"I went back and said to Uncle Emsley: 'Did you
say a sheep man?'

"'I said a sheep man,' says Uncle again. 'You
must have heard tell of Jackson Bird. He's got eight
sections of grazing and four thousand head of the finest
Merinos south of the Arctic Circle.'

"I went out and sat on the ground in the shade of
the store and leaned against a prickly pear. I sifted
sand into my boots with unthinking hands while I solil-
oquised a quantity about this bird with the Jackson
plumage to his name.

"I never had believed in harming sheep men. I see
one, one day, reading a Latin grammar on hossback,
and I never touched him! They never irritated me like
they do most cowmen. You wouldn't go to work now,
and impair and disfigure snoozers, would you, that eat
on tables and wear little shoes and speak to you on subjects? I had always let 'em pass, just as you would a
jack-rabbit; with a polite word and a guess about the
weather, but no stopping to swap canteens. I never
thought it was worth while to be hostile with a snoozer.
And because I'd been lenient, and let 'em live, here was
one going around riding with Miss Willella Learight!

"An hour by sun they come loping back, and stopped at Uncle Emsley's gate. The sheep person helped her off; and they stood throwing each other sentences all sprightful and sagacious for a while. And then this feathered Jackson flies up in his saddle and raises his little stewpot of a hat, and trots off in the direction of his mutton ranch. By this time I had turned the sand out of my boots and unpinned myself from the prickly pear; and by the time he gets half a mile out of Pimienta, I singlefoots up beside him on my bronc.

"I said that snoozer was pink-eyed, but he wasn't. His seeing arrangement was grey enough, but his eye-lashes was pink and his hair was sandy, and that gave you the idea. Sheep man? — he wasn't more than a lamb man, anyhow — a little thing with his neck involved in a yellow silk handkerchief, and shoes tied up in bowknots.

"'Afternoon!' says I to him. 'You now ride with a equestrian who is commonly called Dead-Moral-Certainty Judson, on account of the way I shoot. When I want a stranger to know me I always introduce myself before the draw, for I never did like to shake hands with ghosts.'

"'Ah,' says he, just like that —'Ah, I'm glad to know you, Mr. Judson. I'm Jackson Bird, from over at Mired Mule Ranch.'

"Just then one of my eyes saw a roadrunner skipping down the hill with a young tarantula in his bill, and the other eye noticed a rabbit-hawk sitting on a dead limb in a water-elm. I popped over one after the other with my forty-five, just to show him. 'Two out of three,' says I. 'Birds just naturally seem to draw my fire wherever I go.'

" ' Nice shooting,' says the sheep man, without a flutter. ' But don't you sometimes ever miss the third shot? Elegant fine rain that was last week for the young grass, Mr. Judson? ' says he.

" ' Willie,' says I, riding over close to his palfrey, ' your infatuated parents may have denounced you by the name of Jackson, but you sure moulted into a twittering Willie — let us slough off this here analysis of rain and the elements, and get down to talk that is outside the vocabulary of parrots. That is a bad habit you have got of riding with young ladies over at Pimienta. I've known birds,' says I, ' to be served on toast for less than that. Miss Willella,' says I, ' don't ever want any nest made out of sheep's wool by a tomtit of the Jacksonian branch of ornithology. Now, are you going to quit, or do you wish for to gallop up against this Dead-Moral-Certainty attachment to my name, which is good for two hyphens and at least one set of funeral obsequies? '

" Jackson Bird flushed up some, and then he laughed.

" ' Why, Mr. Judson,' says he, ' you've got the wrong idea. I've called on Miss Learight a few times ; but not for the purpose you imagine. My object is purely a gastronomical one.'

" I reached for my gun.

" ' Any coyote,' says I, ' that would boast of dishonourable —'

" 'Wait a minute,' says this Bird, 'till I explain. What would I do with a wife? If you ever saw that ranch of mine! I do my own cooking and mending. Eating — that's all the pleasure I get out of sheep raising. Mr. Judson, did you ever taste the pancakes that Miss Learight makes?'

" 'Me? No,' I told him. 'I never was advised that she was up to any culinary manœuvres.'

" 'They're golden sunshine,' says he, 'honey-browned by the ambrosial fires of Epicurus. I'd give two years of my life to get the recipe for making them pancakes. That's what I went to see Miss Learight for,' says Jackson Bird, 'but I haven't been able to get it from her. It's an old recipe that's been in the family for seventy-five years. They hand it down from one generation to another, but they don't give it away to outsiders. If I could get that recipe, so I could make them pancakes for myself on my ranch, I'd be a happy man,' says Bird.

" 'Are you sure,' I says to him, 'that it ain't the hand that mixes the pancakes that you're after?'

" 'Sure,' says Jackson. 'Miss Learight is a mighty nice girl, but I can assure you my intentions go no further than the gastro —' but he seen my hand going down to my holster and he changed his similitude — 'than the desire to procure a copy of the pancake recipe,' he finishes.

" 'You ain't such a bad little man,' says I, trying to be fair. 'I was thinking some of making orphans of your sheep, but I'll let you fly away this time. But you

stick to pancakes,' says I, ' as close as the middle one
of a stack; and don't go and mistake sentiments for
syrup, or there'll be singing at your ranch, and you
won't hear it.

" ' To convince you that I am sincere,' says the sheep
man, ' I'll ask you to help me. Miss Learight and you
being closer friends, maybe she would do for you what
she wouldn't for me. If you will get me a copy of that
pancake recipe, I give you my word that I'll never call
upon her again.'

" ' That's fair,' I says, and I shook hands with Jackson Bird. ' I'll get it for you if I can, and glad to
oblige.' And he turned off down the big pear flat on
the Piedra, in the direction of Mired Mule; and I
steered northwest for old Bill Toomey's ranch.

" It was five days afterward when I got another
chance to ride over to Pimienta. Miss Willella and me
passed a gratifying evening at Uncle Emsley's. She
sang some, and exasperated the piano quite a lot with
quotations from the operas. I gave imitations of a
rattlesnake, and told her about Snaky McFee's new way
of skinning cows, and described the trip I made to Saint
Louis once. We was getting along in one another's
estimations fine. Thinks I, if Jackson Bird can now
be persuaded to migrate, I win. I recollect his promise
about the pancake receipt, and I thinks I will persuade
it from Miss Willella and give it to him; and then if I
catches Birdie off of Mired Mule again, I'll make him
hop the twig.

" So, along about ten o'clock, I put on a wheedling

smile and says to Miss Willella: 'Now, if there's any-thing I do like better than the sight of a red steer on green grass it's the taste of a nice hot pancake smoth-ered in sugar-house molasses.'

" Miss Willella gives a little jump on the piano stool, and looked at me curious.

" ' Yes,' says she, ' they're real nice. What did you say was the name of that street in Saint Louis, Mr. Odom, where you lost your hat?'

" ' Pancake Avenue,' says I, with a wink, to show her that I was on about the family receipt, and couldn't be side-corralled off of the subject. 'Come, now, Miss Willella,' I says; ' let's hear how you make 'em. Pan-cakes is just whirling in my head like wagon wheels. Start her off, now — pound of flour, eight dozen eggs, and so on. How does the catalogue of constituents run?'

" ' Excuse me for a moment, please,' says Miss Will-ella, and she gives me a quick kind of sideways look, and slides off the stool. She ambled out into the other room, and directly Uncle Emsley comes in in his shirt sleeves, with a pitcher of water. He turns around to get a glass on the table, and I see a forty-five in his hip pocket. ' Great post-holes!' thinks I, ' but here's a family thinks a heap of cooking receipts, protecting it with firearms. I've known outfits that wouldn't do that much by a family feud.'

" ' Drink this here down,' says Uncle Emsley, hand-ing me the glass of water. ' You've rid too far to-day,

Jud, and got yourself over-excited. Try to think about something else now.'

" ' Do you know how to make them pancakes, Uncle Emsley? ' I asked.

" ' Well, I'm not as apprised in the anatomy of them as some,' says Uncle Emsley, ' but I reckon you take a sifter of plaster of paris and a little dough and saleratus and corn meal, and mix 'em with eggs and buttermilk as usual. Is old Bill going to ship beeves to Kansas City again this spring, Jud? '

" That was all the pancake specifications I could get that night. I didn't wonder that Jackson Bird found it uphill work. So I dropped the subject and talked with Uncle Emsley a while about hollow-horn and cyclones. And then Miss Willella came and said ' Goodnight,' and I hit the breeze for the ranch.

" About a week afterward I met Jackson Bird riding out of Pimienta as I rode in, and we stopped in the road for a few frivolous remarks.

" ' Got the bill of particulars for them flapjacks yet? ' I asked him.

" ' Well, no,' says Jackson. ' I don't seem to have any success in getting hold of it. Did you try? '

" ' I did,' says I, ' and 'twas like trying to dig a prairie dog out of his hole with a peanut hull. That pancake receipt must be a jookalorum, the way they hold on to it.'

" ' I'm most ready to give it up,' says Jackson, so discouraged in his pronunciations that I felt sorry for him;

' but I did want to know how to make them pancakes to eat on my lonely ranch,' says he. ' I lie awake at nights thinking how good they are.'

" ' You keep on trying for it,' I tells him, ' and I'll do the same. One of us is bound to get a rope over its horns before long. Well, so-long, Jacksy.'

" You see, by this time we was on the peacefullest of terms. When I saw that he wasn't after Miss Willella I had more endurable contemplations of that sandy-haired snoozer. In order to help out the ambitions of his appetite I kept on trying to get that receipt from Miss Willella. But every time I would say ' pan-cakes ' she would get sort of remote and fidgety about the eye, and try to change the subject. If I held her to it she would slide out and round up Uncle Emsley with his pitcher of water and hip-pocket howitzer.

" One day I galloped over to the store with a fine bunch of blue verbenas that I cut out of a herd of wild flowers over on Poisoned Dog Prairie. Uncle Emsley looked at 'em with one eye shut and says:

" ' Haven't ye heard the news? '

" ' Cattle up? ' I asks.

" ' Willella and Jackson Bird was married in Pales-tine yesterday,' says he. ' Just got a letter this morn-ing.'

" I dropped them flowers in a cracker-barrel, and let the news trickle in my ears and down toward my upper left-hand shirt pocket until it got to my feet.

" ' Would you mind saying that over again once more, Uncle Emsley? ' says I. ' Maybe my hearing has got wrong, and you only said that prime heifers was 4.80 on the hoof, or something like that.'

" ' Married yesterday,' says Uncle Emsley, ' and gone to Waco and Niagara Falls on a wedding tour. Why, didn't you see none of the signs all along? Jackson Bird has been courting Willella ever since that day he took her out riding.'

" ' Then,' says I, in a kind of yell, ' what was all this zizzaparoola he gives me about pancakes? Tell me *that*.'

" When I said ' pancakes ' Uncle Emsley sort of dodged and stepped back.

" ' Somebody's been dealing me pancakes from the bottom of the deck,' I says, ' and I'll find out. I believe you know. Talk up,' says I, ' or we'll mix a panful of batter right here.'

" I slid over the counter after Uncle Emsley. He grabbed at his gun, but it was in a drawer, and he missed it two inches. I got him by the front of his shirt and shoved him in a corner.

" ' Talk pancakes,' says I, ' or be made into one. Does Miss Willella make 'em? '

" ' She never made one in her life and I never saw one,' says Uncle Emsley, soothing. ' Calm down now, Jud — calm down. You've got excited, and that wound in your head is contaminating your sense of intelligence. Try not to think about pancakes.'

" ' Uncle Emsley,' says I, ' I'm not wounded in the head except so far as my natural cogitative instincts run to runts. Jackson Bird told me he was calling on Miss Willella for the purpose of finding out her system

of producing pancakes, and he asked me to help him
get the bill of lading of the ingredients. I done so, with
the results as you see. Have I been sodded down with
Johnson grass by a pink-eyed snoozer, or what?'

" ' Slack up your grip on my dress shirt,' says Uncle
Emsley, ' and I'll tell you. Yes, it looks like Jackson
Bird has gone and humbugged you some. The day after
he went riding with Willella he came back and told me
and her to watch out for you whenever you got to talking about pancakes. He said you was in camp once
where they was cooking flapjacks, and one of the fellows cut you over the head with a frying pan. Jackson
said that whenever you got overhot or excited that
wound hurt you and made you kind of crazy, and you
went raving about pancakes. He told us to just get you
worked off of the subject and soothed down, and you
wouldn't be dangerous. So, me and Willella done the
best by you we knew how. Well, well,' says Uncle Emsley, ' that Jackson Bird is sure a seldom kind of a
snoozer.' "

During the progress of Jud's story he had been slowly
but deftly combining certain portions of the contents of
his sacks and cans. Toward the close of it he set before
me the finished product — a pair of red-hot, rich-hued
pancakes on a tin plate. From some secret hoarding
place he also brought a lump of excellent butter and a
bottle of golden syrup.

" How long ago did these things happen? " I asked
him.

" Three years," said Jud. " They're living on the

Mired Mule Ranch now. But I haven't seen either of 'em since. They say Jackson Bird was fixing his ranch up fine with rocking chairs and window curtains all the time he was putting me up the pancake tree. Oh, I got over it after a while. But the boys kept the racket up."

" Did you make these cakes by the famous recipe? " I asked.

" Didn't I tell you there wasn't no receipt? " said Jud. " The boys hollered pancakes till they got pancake hungry, and I cut this recipe out of a newspaper. How does the truck taste? "

" They're delicious," I answered. " Why don't you have some, too, Jud? "

I was sure I heard a sigh.

" Me? " said Jud. " I don't never eat 'em."

THE REFORMATION OF CALLIOPE

CALLIOPE CATESBY was in his humours again. Ennui was upon him. This goodly promontory, the earth — particularly that portion of it known as Quicksand — was to him no more than a pestilent congregation of vapours. Overtaken by the megrims, the philosopher may seek relief in soliloquy; my lady find solace in tears; the flaccid Easterner scold at the millinery bills of his women folk. Such recourse was insufficient to the denizens of Quicksand. Calliope, especially, was wont to express his ennui according to his lights.

Over night Calliope had hung out signals of approaching low spirits. He had kicked his own dog on the porch of the Occidental Hotel, and refused to apologise. He had become capricious and fault-finding in conversation. While strolling about he reached often for twigs of mesquite and chewed the leaves fiercely. That was always an ominous act. Another symptom alarming to those who were familiar with the different stages of his doldrums was his increasing politeness and a tendency to use formal phrases. A husky softness succeeded the usual penetrating drawl in his tones. A dangerous courtesy marked his manners. Later, his smile became crooked, the left side of his mouth slanting upward, and Quicksand got ready to stand from under.

At this stage Calliope generally began to drink. Finally, about midnight, he was seen going homeward, saluting those whom he met with exaggerated but inoffensive courtesy. Not yet was Calliope's melancholy at the danger point. He would seat himself at the window of the room he occupied over Silvester's tonsorial parlours and there chant lugubrious and tuneless ballads until morning, accompanying the noises by appropriate maltreatment of a jingling guitar. More magnanimous than Nero, he would thus give musical warning of the forthcoming municipal upheaval that Quicksand was scheduled to endure.

A quiet, amiable man was Calliope Catesby at other times — quiet to indolence, and amiable to worthlessness. At best he was a loafer and a nuisance; at worst he was the Terror of Quicksand. His ostensible occupation was something subordinate in the real estate line; he drove the beguiled Easterner in buckboards out to look over lots and ranch property. Originally he came from one of the Gulf States, his lank six feet, slurring rhythm of speech, and sectional idioms giving evidence of his birthplace.

And yet, after taking on Western adjustments, this languid pine-box whittler, cracker barrel hugger, shady corner lounger of the cotton fields and sumac hills of the South became famed as a bad man among men who had made a life-long study of the art of truculence.

At nine the next morning Calliope was fit. Inspired

by his own barbarous melodies and the contents of his jug, he was ready primed to gather fresh laurels from the diffident brow of Quicksand. Encircled and criss-crossed with cartridge belts, abundantly garnished with revolvers, and copiously drunk, he poured forth into Quicksand's main street. Too chivalrous to surprise and capture a town by silent sortie, he paused at the nearest corner and emitted his slogan — that fearful, brassy yell, so reminiscent of the steam piano, that had gained for him the classic appellation that had super-seded his own baptismal name. Following close upon his vociferation came three shots from his forty-five by way of limbering up the guns and testing his aim. A yellow dog, the personal property of Colonel Swazey, the proprietor of the Occidental, fell feet upward in the dust with one farewell yelp. A Mexican who was crossing the street from the Blue Front grocery carry-ing in his hand a bottle of kerosene, was stimulated to a sudden and admirable burst of speed, still grasping the neck of the shattered bottle. The new gilt weather-cock on Judge Riley's lemon and ultramarine two-story residence shivered, flapped, and hung by a splinter, the sport of the wanton breezes.

The artillery was in trim. Calliope's hand was steady. The high, calm ecstasy of habitual battle was upon him, though slightly embittered by the sadness of Alexander in that his conquests were limited to the small world of Quicksand.

Down the street went Calliope, shooting right and left. Glass fell like hail; dogs vamosed; chickens flew, squawking; feminine voices shrieked concernedly to youngsters at large. The din was perforated at intervals by the *staccato* of the Terror's guns, and was drowned periodically by the brazen screech that Quicksand knew so well. The occasions of Calliope's low spirits were legal holidays in Quicksand. All along the main street in advance of his coming clerks were putting up shutters and closing doors. Business would languish for a space. The right of way was Calliope's, and as he advanced, observing the dearth of opposition and the few opportunities for distraction, his ennui perceptibly increased.

But some four squares farther down lively preparations were being made to minister to Mr. Catesby's love for interchange of compliments and repartee. On the previous night numerous messengers had hastened to advise Buck Patterson, the city marshal, of Calliope's impending eruption. The patience of that official, often strained in extending leniency toward the disturber's misdeeds, had been overtaxed. In Quicksand some indulgence was accorded the natural ebullition of human nature. Providing that the lives of the more useful citizens were not recklessly squandered, or too much property needlessly laid waste, the community sentiment was against a too strict enforcement of the law. But Calliope had raised the limit. His outbursts had been too frequent and too violent to come within the classification of a normal and sanitary relaxation of spirit.

Buck Patterson had been expecting and awaiting in his little ten-by-twelve frame office that preliminary yell announcing that Calliope was feeling blue. When the signal came the City Marshal rose to his feet and buckled on his guns. Two deputy sheriffs and three citizens who had proven the edible qualities of fire also stood up, ready to bandy with Calliope's leaden jocularities.

"Gather that fellow in," said Buck Patterson, setting forth the lines of the campaign. "Don't have no talk, but shoot as soon as you can get a show. Keep behind cover and bring him down. He's a nogood 'un. It's up to Calliope to turn up his toes this time, I reckon. Go to him all spraddled out, boys. And don't git too reckless, for what Calliope shoots at he hits."

Buck Patterson, tall, muscular, and solemn-faced, with his bright "City Marshal" badge shining on the breast of his blue flannel shirt, gave his posse directions for the onslaught upon Calliope. The plan was to accomplish the downfall of the Quicksand Terror without loss to the attacking party, if possible.

The splenetic Calliope, unconscious of retributive plots, was steaming down the channel, cannonading on either side, when he suddenly became aware of breakers ahead. The city marshal and one of the deputies rose up behind some dry-goods boxes half a square to the front and opened fire. At the same time the rest of the posse, divided, shelled him from two side streets up which they were cautiously manœuvring from a well-executed detour.

The first volley broke the lock of one of Calliope's guns, cut a neat underbit in his right ear, and exploded a cartridge in his crossbelt, scorching his ribs as it burst. Feeling braced up by this unexpected tonic to his spiritual depression, Calliope executed a fortissimo note from his upper register, and returned the fire like an echo. The upholders of the law dodged at his flash, but a trifle too late to save one of the deputies a bullet just above the elbow, and the marshal a bleeding cheek from a splinter that a ball tore from the box he had ducked behind.

And now Calliope met the enemy's tactics in kind. Choosing with a rapid eye the street from which the weakest and least accurate fire had come, he invaded it at a double-quick, abandoning the unprotected middle of the street. With rare cunning the opposing force in that direction — one of the deputies and two of the valorous volunteers — waited, concealed by beer barrels, until Calliope had passed their retreat, and then peppered him from the rear. In another moment they were reinforced by the marshal and his other men, and then Calliope felt that in order to successfully prolong the delights of the controversy he must find some means of reducing the great odds against him. His eye fell upon a structure that seemed to hold out this promise, providing he could reach it.

Not far away was the little railroad station, its building a strong box house, ten by twenty feet, resting upon a platform four feet above ground. Windows were in each of its walls. Something like a fort it might become to a man thus sorely pressed by superior numbers.

Calliope made a bold and rapid spurt for it, the mar

shal's crowd " smoking " him as he ran. He reached
the haven in safety, the station agent leaving the building by a window, like a flying squirrel, as the garrison
entered the door.

Patterson and his supporters halted under protection of a pile of lumber and held consultations. In the
station was an unterrified desperado who was an excellent
shot and carried an abundance of ammunition. For
thirty yards on each side of the besieged was a stretch of
bare, open ground. It was a sure thing that the man
who attempted to enter that unprotected area would be
stopped by one of Calliope's bullets.

The city marshal was resolved. He had decided that
Calliope Catesby should no more wake the echoes of
Quicksand with his strident whoop. He had so an-
nounced. Officially and personally he felt imperatively
bound to put the soft pedal on that instrument of dis-
cord. It played bad tunes.

Standing near was a hand truck used in the ma-
nipulation of small freight. It stood by a shed full of
sacked wool, a consignment from one of the sheep
ranches. On this truck the marshal and his men piled
three heavy sacks of wool. Stooping low, Buck Patterson started for Calliope's fort, slowly pushing this
loaded truck before him for protection. The posse,
scattering broadly, stood ready to nip the besieged in
case he should show himself in an effort to repel the
juggernaut of justice that was creeping upon him.
Only once did Calliope make demonstration. He fired
from a window, and some tufts of wool spurted from the

marshal's trustworthy bulwark. The return shots from the posse pattered against the window frame of the fort. No loss resulted on either side.

The marshal was too deeply engrossed in steering his protected battleship to be aware of the approach of the morning train until he was within a few feet of the platform. The train was coming up on the other side of it. It stopped only one minute at Quicksand. What an opportunity it would offer to Calliope! He had only to step out the other door, mount the train, and away.

Abandoning his breastworks, Buck, with his gun ready, dashed up the steps and into the room, driving open the closed door with one heave of his weighty shoulder. The members of the posse heard one shot fired inside, and then there was silence.

At length the wounded man opened his eyes. After a blank space he again could see and hear and feel and think. Turning his eyes about, he found himself lying on a wooden bench. A tall man with a perplexed countenance, wearing a big badge with "City Marshal" engraved upon it, stood over him. A little old woman in black, with a wrinkled face and sparkling black eyes, was holding a wet handkerchief against one of his temples. He was trying to get these facts fixed in his mind and connected with past events, when the old woman began to talk.

"There now, great, big, strong man! That bullet never tetched ye! Jest skeeted along the side of your head and sort of paralysed ye for a spell. I've heerd

"There now, great, big strong man! That bullet never tetched ye!"

of sech things afore; cun-cussion is what they names
it. Abel Wadkins used to kill squirrels that way —
barkin' 'em, Abe called it. You jest been barked, sir,
and you'll be all right in a little bit. Feel lots better
already, don't ye! You just lay still a while longer
and let me bathe your head. You don't know me, I
reckon, and 'tain't surprisin' that you shouldn't. I come
in on that train from Alabama to see my son. Big son,
ain't he? Lands! you wouldn't hardly think he'd ever
been a baby, would ye? This is my son, sir."

Half turning, the old woman looked up at the standing man, her worn face lighting with a proud and wonderful smile. She reached out one veined and calloused
hand and took one of her son's. Then smiling cheerily
down at the prostrate man, she continued to dip the
handkerchief, in the waiting-room tin washbasin and
gently apply it to his temple. She had the benevolent
garrulity of old age.

"I ain't seen my son before," she continued, "in
eight years. One of my nephews, Elkanah Price, he's
a conductor on one of them railroads and he got me
a pass to come out here. I can stay a whole week on
it, and then it'll take me back again. Jest think, now,
that little boy of mine has got to be a officer — a city
marshal of a whole town! That's somethin' like a con-
stable, ain't it? I never knowed he was a officer; he
didn't say nothin' about it in his letters. I reckon he
thought his old mother'd be skeered about the danger he
was in. But, laws! I never was much of a hand to git
skeered. 'Tain't no use. I heard them guns a-shootin'

135

while I was gittin' off them cars, and I see smoke a-comin' out of the depot, but I jest walked right along. Then I see son's face lookin' out through the window. I knowed him at oncet. He met me at the door, and squeezed me 'most to death. And there you was, sir, a-lyin' there jest like you was dead, and I 'lowed we'd see what might be done to help sot you up."

" I think I'll sit up now," said the concussion patient. " I'm feeling pretty fair by this time."

He sat, somewhat weakly yet, leaning against the wall. He was a rugged man, big-boned and straight. His eyes, steady and keen, seemed to linger upon the face of the man standing so still above him. His look wandered often from the face he studied to the marshal's badge upon the other's breast.

" Yes, yes, you'll be all right," said the old woman, patting his arm, " if you don't get to cuttin' up agin, and havin' folks shootin' at you. Son told me about you, sir, while you was layin' senseless on the floor. Don't you take it as meddlesome fer an old woman with a son as big as you to talk about it. And you mustn't hold no grudge ag'in' my son for havin' to shoot at ye. A officer has got to take up for the law — it's his duty — and them that acts bad and lives wrong has to suffer. Don't blame my son any, sir —'tain't his fault. He's always been a good boy — good when he was growin' up, and kind and 'bedient and well-behaved. Won't you let me advise you, sir, not to do so no more? Be a good man, and leave liquor alone and live peaceably and godly.

Keep away from bad company and work honest and sleep sweet."

The black-mittened hand of the old pleader gently touched the breast of the man she addressed. Very earnest and candid her old, worn face looked. In her rusty black dress and antique bonnet she sat, near the close of a long life, and epitomised the experience of the world. Still the man to whom she spoke gazed above her head, contemplating the silent son of the old mother.

"What does the marshal say?" he asked. "Does he believe the advice is good? Suppose the marshal speaks up and says if the talk's all right?"

The tall man moved uneasily. He fingered the badge on his breast for a moment, and then he put an arm around the old woman and drew her close to him. She smiled the unchanging mother smile of three-score years, and patted his big brown hand with her crooked, mittened fingers while her son spake.

"I says this," he said, looking squarely into the eyes of the other man, "that if I was in your place I'd follow it. If I was a drunken, desp'rate character, without shame or hope, I'd follow it. If I was in your place and you was in mine I'd say: 'Marshal, I'm willin' tc swear if you'll give me the chance I'll quit the racket. I'll drop the tanglefoot and the gun play, and won't play hoss no more. I'll be a good citizen and go to work and quit my foolishness. So help me God!' That's what I'd say to you if you was marshal and I was in your place.'"

"Hear my son talkin'," said the old woman softly. "Hear him, sir. You promise to be good and he won't do you no harm. Forty-one year ago his heart first beat ag'in' mine, and it's beat true ever since."

The other man rose to his feet, trying his limbs and stretching his muscles.

"Then," said he, "if you was in my place and said that, and I was marshal, I'd say: 'Go free, and do your best to keep your promise.'"

"Lawsy!" exclaimed the old woman, in a sudden flutter, "ef I didn't clear forget that trunk of mine! I see a man settin' it on the platform jest as I seen son's face in the window, and it went plum out of my head. There's eight jars of home-made quince jam in that trunk that I made myself. I wouldn't have nothin' happen to them jars for a red apple."

Away to the door she trotted, spry and anxious, and then Calliope Catesby spoke out to Buck Patterson:

"I just couldn't help it, Buck. I seen her through the window a-comin' in. She never had heard a word 'bout my tough ways. I didn't have the nerve to let her know I was a worthless cuss bein' hunted down by the community. There you was lyin' where my shot laid you, like you was dead. The idea struck me sudden, and I just took your badge off and fastened it onto myself, and I fastened my reputation onto you. I told her I was the marshal and you was a holy terror. You can take your badge back now, Buck."

With shaking fingers Calliope began to unfasten the disc of metal from his shirt.

138

" Easy there! " said Buck Patterson. " You keep that badge right where it is, Calliope Catesby. Don't you dare to take it off till the day your mother leaves this town. You'll be city marshal of Quicksand as long as she's here to know it. After I stir around town a bit and put 'em on I'll guarantee that nobody won't give the thing away to her. And say, you leather-headed, rip-roarin', low-down son of a locoed cyclone, you follow that advice she give me! I'm goin' to take some of it myself, too."

" Buck," said Calliope feelingly, " ef I don't I hope I may —"

" Shut up," said Buck. " She's a-comin' back."

THE END

CAUGHT

THE plans for the detention of the flying President Miraflores and his companion at the coast line seemed hardly likely to fail. Dr. Zavalla himself had gone to the port of Alazan to establish a guard at that point. At Coralio the Liberal patriot Varras could be depended upon to keep close watch. Goodwin held himself responsible for the district about Coralio.

The news of the president's flight had been disclosed to no one in the coast towns save trusted members of the ambitious political party that was desirous of succeeding to power. The telegraph wire running from San Mateo to the coast had been cut far up on the mountain trail by an emissary of Zavalla's. Long before this could be repaired and word received along it from the capital the fugitives would have reached the coast and the question of escape or capture been solved.

Goodwin had stationed armed sentinels at frequent intervals along the shore for a mile in each direction from Coralio. They were instructed to keep a vigilant lookout during the night to prevent Miraflores from attempting to embark stealthily by means of some boat or sloop found by chance at the water's edge. A dozen patrols walked the streets of Coralio unsuspected, ready to intercept the truant official should he show himself there.

Goodwin was very well convinced that no precautions had been overlooked. He strolled about the streets that bore such high-sounding names and were but narrow, grass-covered lanes, lending his own aid to the vigil that had been intrusted to him by Bob Englehart.

The town had begun the tepid round of its nightly diversions. A few leisurely dandies, clad in white duck, with flowing neckties, and swinging slim bamboo canes, threaded the grassy by-ways toward the houses of their favoured señoritas. Those who wooed the art of music dragged tirelessly at whining concertinas, or fingered lugubrious guitars at doors and windows. An occasional soldier from the *cuartel*, with flapping straw hat, without coat or shoes, hurried by, balancing his long gun like a lance in one hand. From every density of the foliage the giant tree frogs sounded their loud and irritating clatter.

Further out, where the by-ways perished at the brink
of the jungle, the guttural cries of marauding bab-
oons and the coughing of the alligators in the black
estuaries fractured the vain silence of the wood.

By ten o'clock the streets were deserted. The oil
lamps that had burned, a sickly yellow, at random
corners, had been extinguished by some economical
civic agent. Coralio lay sleeping calmly between top-
pling mountains and encroaching sea like a stolen
babe in the arms of its abductors. Somewhere over
in that tropical darkness — perhaps already thread-
ing the profundities of the alluvial lowlands — the
high adventurer and his mate were moving toward
land's end. The game of Fox-in-the-Morning
should be coming soon to its close.

Goodwin, at his deliberate gait, passed the long,
low *cuartel* where Coralio's contingent of Anchuria's
military force slumbered, with its bare toes pointed
heavenward. There was a law that no civilian
might come so near the headquarters of that citadel
of war after nine o'clock, but Goodwin was always
forgetting the minor statutes.

" *Quién vive?* " shrieked the sentinel, wrestling
prodigiously with his lengthy musket.

" *Americano,* " growled Goodwin, without turning
his head, and passed on, unhalted.

To the right he turned, and to the left up the street that ultimately reached the Plaza Nacional. When within the toss of a cigar stump from the intersecting Street of the Holy Sepulchre, he stopped suddenly in the pathway.

He saw the form of a tall man, clothed in black and carrying a large valise, hurry down the cross-street in the direction of the beach. And Goodwin's second glance made him aware of a woman at the man's elbow on the farther side, who seemed to urge forward, if not even to assist, her companion in their swift but silent progress. They were no Coralians, those two.

Goodwin followed at increased speed, but without any of the artful tactics that are so dear to the heart of the sleuth. The American was too broad to feel the instinct of the detective. He stood as an agent for the people of Anchuria, and but for political reasons he would have demanded then and there the money. It was the design of his party to secure the imperilled fund, to restore it to the treasury of the country, and to declare itself in power without bloodshed or resistance.

The couple halted at the door of the Hotel de los Estranjeros, and the man struck upon the wood with the impatience of one unused to his entry being stayed. Madama was long in response; but after a time her light showed, the door was opened, and the guests housed.

Goodwin stood in the quiet street, lighting another cigar. In two minutes a faint gleam began to show between the slats of the jalousies in the upper story of the hotel. "They have engaged rooms," said Goodwin to himself. "So, then, their arrangements for sailing have yet to be made."

At that moment there came along one Estebán Delgado, a barber, an enemy to existing government, a jovial plotter against stagnation in any form. This barber was one of Coralio's saddest dogs, often remaining out of doors as late as eleven, post meridian. He was a partisan Liberal; and he greeted Goodwin with flatulent importance as a brother in the cause. But he had something important to tell.

"What think you, Don Frank!" he cried, in the universal tone of the conspirator. "I have to-night shaved *la barba* — what you call the 'weeskers' of the *Presidente* himself, of this countree! Consider! He sent for me to come. In the poor *casita* of an old woman he awaited me — in a verree leetle house in a dark place. *Carramba!* — el Señor Presidente to make himself thus secret and obscured! I think he desired not to be known — but, *carajo!* can you shave a man and not see his face? This gold piece he gave me, and said it was to be all quite still. I think, Don Frank, there is what you call a chip over the bug."

" Have you ever seen President Miraflores before? " asked Goodwin.

" But once," answered Estebán. " He is tall; and he had weeskers, verree black and sufficient."

" Was anyone else present when you shaved him? "

" An old Indian woman, Señor, that belonged with the *casa*, and one señorita — a ladee of so much beautee! — *ah, Dios!* "

" All right, Estebán," said Goodwin. " It's very lucky that you happened along with your tonsorial information. The new administration will be likely to remember you for this."

Then in a few words he made the barber acquainted with the crisis into which the affairs of the nation had culminated, and instructed him to remain outside, keeping watch upon the two sides of the hotel that looked upon the street, and observing whether anyone should attempt to leave the house by any door or window. Goodwin himself went to the door through which the guests had entered, opened it and stepped inside.

Madama had returned downstairs from her journey above to see after the comfort of her lodgers. Her candle stood upon the bar. She was about to take a thimbleful of rum as a solace for having her rest disturbed. She looked up without surprise or alarm as her third caller entered.

"Ah! it is the Señor Goodwin. Not often does he honour my poor house by his presence."

"I must come oftener," said Goodwin, with the Goodwin smile. "I hear that your cognac is the best between Belize to the north and Rio to the south. Set out the bottle, Madama, and let us have the proof in *un vasito* for each of us."

"My *aguardiente*," said Madama, with pride, "is the best. It grows, in beautiful bottles, in the dark places among the banana-trees. *Si, Señor.* Only at midnight can they be picked by sailor-men who bring them, before daylight comes, to your back door. Good *aguardiente* is a verree difficult fruit to handle, Señor Goodwin."

Smuggling, in Coralio, was much nearer than competition to being the life of trade. One spoke of it slyly, yet with a certain conceit, when it had been well accomplished.

"You have guests in the house to-night," said Goodwin, laying a silver dollar upon the counter.

"Why not?" said Madama, counting the change. "Two; but the smallest while finished to arrive. One señor, not quite old, and one señorita of sufficient handsomeness. To their rooms they have ascended, not desiring the to-eat nor the to-drink. Two rooms — *Numero* 9 and *Numero* 10."

"I was expecting that gentleman and that lady," said Goodwin. "I have important *negocios* that must be transacted. Will you allow me to see them?"

"Why not?" sighed Madama, placidly. "Why should not Señor Goodwin ascend and speak to his friends? *Está bueno*. Room *Numero* 9 and room *Numero* 10."

Goodwin loosened in his coat pocket the American revolver that he carried, and ascended the steep, dark stairway.

In the hallway above, the saffron light from a hanging lamp allowed him to select the gaudy numbers on the doors. He turned the knob of Number 9, entered and closed the door behind him.

If that was Isabel Guilbert seated by the table in that poorly furnished room, report had failed to do her charms justice. She rested her head upon one hand. Extreme fatigue was signified in every line of her figure; and upon her countenance a deep perplexity was written. Her eyes were gray-irised, and of that mould that seems to have belonged to the orbs of all the famous queens of hearts. Their whites were singularly clear and brilliant, concealed above the irises by heavy horizontal lids, and showing a snowy line below them. Such eyes denote great nobility, vigour, and, if you can conceive of it, a most generous selfishness. She looked up when the American entered, with an expression of surprised inquiry, but without alarm.

Goodwin took off his hat and seated himself, with his characteristic deliberate ease, upon a corner of the table. He held a lighted cigar between his fingers. He took this familiar course because he was sure that preliminaries would be wasted upon Miss Guilbert. He knew her history, and the small part that the conventions had played in it.

"Good evening," he said. "Now, madame, let us come to business at once. You will observe that I mention no names, but I know who is in the next room, and what he carries in that valise. That is the point which brings me here. I have come to dictate terms of surrender."

The lady neither moved nor replied, but steadily regarded the cigar in Goodwin's hand.

"We," continued the dictator, thoughtfully re-

garding the neat buckskin shoe on his gently swinging foot —" I speak for a considerable majority of
the people — demand the return of the stolen funds
belonging to them. Our terms go very little further
than that. They are very simple. As an accred-
ited spokesman, I promise that our interference will
cease if they are accepted. Give up the money, and
you and your companion will be permitted to pro-
ceed wherever you will. In fact, assistance will be
given you in the matter of securing a passage by any
outgoing vessel you may choose. It is on my personal responsibility that I add congratulations to the
gentleman in Number 10 upon his taste in feminine
charms."

Returning his cigar to his mouth, Goodwin observed her, and saw that her eyes followed it and
rested upon it with icy and significant concentration.
Apparently she had not heard a word he had said.
He understood, tossed the cigar out the window,
and, with an amused laugh, slid from the table to
his feet.

" That is better," said the lady. " It makes it
possible for me to listen to you. For a second lesson
in good manners, you might now tell me by whom I
am being insulted."

" I am sorry," said Goodwin, leaning one hand on

the table, "that my time is too brief for devoting much of it to a course of etiquette. Come, now; I appeal to your good sense. You have shown yourself, in more than one instance, to be well aware of what is to your advantage. This is an occasion that demands the exercise of your undoubted intelligence. There is no mystery here. I am Frank Goodwin; and I have come for the money. I entered this room at a venture. Had I entered the other I would have had it before now. Do you want it in words? The gentleman in Number 10 has betrayed a great trust. He has robbed his people of a large sum, and it is I who will prevent their losing it. I do not say who that gentleman is; but if I should be forced to see him and he should prove to be a certain high official of the republic, it will be my duty to arrest him. The house is guarded. I am offering you liberal terms. It is not absolutely necessary that I confer personally with the gentleman in the next room. Bring me the valise containing the money, and we will call the affair ended."

The lady arose from her chair and stood for a moment, thinking deeply.

"Do you live here, Mr. Goodwin?" she asked, presently.

"Yes."

" What is your authority for this intrusion? "

" I am an instrument of the republic. I was advised by wire of the movements of the — gentleman in Number 10."

" May I ask you two or three questions? I believe you to be a man more apt to be truthful than — timid. What sort of a town is this — Coralio, I think they call it? "

" Not much of a town," said Goodwin, smiling. " A banana town, as they run. Grass huts, 'dobes, five or six two-story houses, accommodations limited, population half-breed Spanish and Indian, Caribs and blackamoors. No sidewalks to speak of, no amusements. Rather unmoral. That's an offhand sketch, of course."

" Are there any inducements, say in a social or in a business way, for people to reside here? "

" Oh, yes," answered Goodwin, smiling broadly. " There are no afternoon teas, no hand-organs, no department stores — and there is no extradition treaty."

" He told me," went on the lady, speaking as if to herself, and with a slight frown, " that there were towns on this coast of beauty and importance; that there was a pleasing social order — especially an American colony of cultured residents."

"There is an American colony," said Goodwin, gazing at her in some wonder. "Some of the members are all right. Some are fugitives from justice from the States. I recall two exiled bank presidents, one army paymaster under a cloud, a couple of manslayers, and a widow — arsenic, I believe, was the suspicion in her case. I myself complete the colony, but, as yet, I have not distinguished myself by any particular crime."

"Do not lose hope," said the lady, dryly; "I see nothing in your actions to-night to guarantee you further obscurity. Some mistake has been made; I do not know just where. But *him* you shall not disturb to-night. The journey has fatigued him so that he has fallen asleep, I think, in his clothes. You talk of stolen money! I do not understand you. Some mistake has been made. I will convince you. Remain where you are and I will bring you the valise that you seem to covet so, and show it to you."

She moved toward the closed door that connected the two rooms, but stopped, and half turned and bestowed upon Goodwin a grave, searching look that ended in a quizzical smile.

"You force my door," she said, "and you follow your ruffianly behaviour with the basest accusations;

and yet "— she hesitated, as if to reconsider what she was about to say —" and yet — it is a puzzling thing — I am sure there has been some mistake."

She took a step toward the door, but Goodwin stayed her by a light touch upon her arm. I have said before that women turned to look at him in the streets. He was the viking sort of man, big, good-looking, and with an air of kindly truculence. She was dark and proud, glowing or pale as her mood moved her. I do not know if Eve were light or dark, but if such a woman had stood in the garden I know that the apple would have been eaten. This woman was to be Goodwin's fate, and he did not know it; but he must have felt the first throes of destiny, for, as he faced her, the knowledge of what report named her turned bitter in his throat.

" If there has been any mistake," he said, hotly, " it was yours. I do not blame the man who has lost his country, his honour, and is about to lose the poor consolation of his stolen riches as much as I blame you, for, by Heaven! I can very well see how he was brought to it. I can understand, and pity him. It is such women as you that strew this de-graded coast with wretched exiles, that make men forget their trusts, that drag —"

The lady interrupted him with a weary gesture.

"There is no need to continue your insults," she said, coldly. "I do not understand what you are saying, nor do I know what mad blunder you are making; but if the inspection of the contents of a gentleman's portmanteau will rid me of you, let us delay it no longer."

She passed quickly and noiselessly into the other room, and returned with the heavy leather valise, which she handed to the American with an air of patient contempt.

Goodwin set the valise quickly upon the table and began to unfasten the straps. The lady stood by, with an expression of infinite scorn and weariness upon her face.

The valise opened wide to a powerful, sidelong wrench. Goodwin dragged out two or three articles of clothing, exposing the bulk of its contents — package after package of tightly packed United States bank and treasury notes of large denomination. Reckoning from the high figures written upon the paper bands that bound them, the total must have come closely upon the hundred thousand mark.

Goodwin glanced swiftly at the woman, and saw, with surprise and a thrill of pleasure that he wondered at, that she had experienced an unmistakable shock. Her eyes grew wide, she gasped, and leaned

heavily against the table. She had been ignorant,
then, he inferred, that her companion had looted the
government treasury. But why, he angrily asked
himself, should he be so well pleased to think this
wandering and unscrupulous singer not so black as
report had painted her?

A noise in the other room startled them both.
The door swung open, and a tall, elderly, dark com-
plexioned man, recently shaven, hurried into the
room.

All the pictures of President Miraflores represent
him as the possessor of a luxuriant supply of dark
and carefully tended whiskers; but the story of the
barber, Estebán, had prepared Goodwin for the
change.

The man stumbled in from the dark room, his eyes
blinking at the lamplight, and heavy from sleep.

"What does this mean?" he demanded in excellent English, with a keen and perturbed look at the
American — "robbery?"

"Very near it," answered Goodwin. "But I
rather think I'm in time to prevent it. I represent
the people to whom this money belongs, and I have
come to convey it back to them." He thrust his
hand into a pocket of his loose, linen coat.

The other man's hand went quickly behind him.

" Don't draw," called Goodwin, sharply ; " I've got you covered from my pocket."

The lady stepped forward, and laid one hand upon the shoulder of her hesitating companion. She pointed to the table. " Tell me the truth — the truth," she said, in a low voice. " Whose money is that? "

The man did not answer. He gave a deep, long-drawn sigh, leaned and kissed her on the forehead, stepped back into the other room and closed the door.

Goodwin foresaw his purpose, and jumped for the door, but the report of the pistol echoed as his hand touched the knob. A heavy fall followed, and some one swept him aside and struggled into the room of the fallen man.

A desolation, thought Goodwin, greater than that derived from the loss of cavalier and gold must have been in the heart of the enchantress to have wrung from her, in that moment, the cry of one turning to the all-forgiving, all-comforting earthly consoler — to have made her call out from that bloody and dishonoured room — " Oh, mother, mother, mother! "

But there was an alarm outside. The barber, Estebán, at the sound of the shot, had raised his voice ; and the shot itself had aroused half the town. A pattering of feet came up the street, and official

orders rang out on the still air. Goodwin had a
duty to perform. Circumstances had made him the
custodian of his adopted country's treasure. Swiftly
cramming the money into the valise, he closed it,
leaned far out of the window and dropped it into a
thick orange-tree in the little inclosure below.

They will tell you in Coralio, as they delight in
telling the stranger, of the conclusion of that tragic
flight. They will tell you how the upholders of the
law came apace when the alarm was sounded — the
Comandante in red slippers and a jacket like a head
waiter's and girded sword, the soldiers with their interminable guns, followed by outnumbering officers
struggling into their gold lace and epaulettes; the
barefooted policemen (the only capables in the lot),
and ruffled citizens of every hue and description.

They say that the countenance of the dead man
was marred sadly by the effects of the shot; but he
was identified as the fallen president by both Goodwin and the barber Estebán. On the next morning
messages began to come over the mended telegraph
wire; and the story of the flight from the capital was
given out to the public. In San Mateo the revolu-
tionary party had seized the sceptre of government,
without opposition, and the *vivas* of the mercurial

"*Swiftly cramming the money into the valise, he closed it, leaned far out of the window and dropped it into a thick orange-tree in the little inclosure below.*"

populace quickly effaced the interest belonging to the unfortunate Miraflores.

They will relate to you how the new government sifted the towns and raked the roads to find the valise containing Anchuria's surplus capital, which the president was known to have carried with him, but all in vain. In Coralio Señor Goodwin himself led the searching party which combed that town as carefully as a woman combs her hair; but the money was not found.

So they buried the dead man, without honours, back of the town near the little bridge that spans the mangrove swamp; and for a *real* a boy will show you his grave. They say that the old woman in whose hut the barber shaved the president placed the wooden slab at his head, and burned the inscription upon it with a hot iron.

You will hear also that Señor Goodwin, like a tower of strength, shielded Doña Isabel Guilbert through those subsequent distressful days; and that his scruples as to her past career (if he had any) vanished; and her adventuresome waywardness (if she had any) left her, and they were wedded and were happy.

The American built a home on a little foot hill near the town. It is a conglomerate structure of native woods that, exported, would be worth a fortune, and of brick, palm, glass, bamboo and adobe. There is a paradise of nature about it; and something of the same sort within. The natives speak of its interior with hands uplifted in admiration. There are floors polished like mirrors and covered with hand-woven Indian rugs of silk fibre, tall ornaments and pictures, musical instruments and papered walls —" figure-it-to-yourself!" they exclaim.

But they cannot tell you in Coralio (as you shall learn) what became of the money that Frank Goodwin dropped into the orange-tree. But that shall come later; for the palms are fluttering in the breeze, bidding us to sport and gaiety.